DELIGHTFULLY OURS

THERESA HODGE

Delightfully Ours

To every reader who supports me time and time again.

Kassidy

"Why do you eat cake like that Kassidy? You already know you're a big girl and can stand to lose some weight."

I pick up the napkin from the table and brush the cake crumbs off my lips. I glare at my boyfriend, Stanley, who is sitting across from me and looking at me with a sign of impatience in his eyes.

"Why don't you tell me what you really think?" I say as I brush a stray piece of wavy natural hair from my face.

"I'm just saying, every time dessert is offered at a restaurant, party, or event, you don't have to accept. I thought you promised me you would lose some weight."

"Stanley, I've been on every fad diet known to man," I explain, thinking that I should order another slice of cake just to wipe that pompous look off his face. It is really depressing listening to my boyfriend complain about me and gloating about how imperfect I am every time we get together. He doesn't know the only thing I had for breakfast this morning was half a grapefruit and a boiled egg without the yoke. I even skipped lunch altogether, but I don't enlighten him of that fact.

Instead I say, "Stanley, you knew I was between a size twelve and fourteen in plus-size clothing when we met two years ago. If you are so turned off by my weight maybe we shouldn't be talking about a future together after all."

"Well, I'm glad you brought that up." Stanley clears his throat before taking a sip of red wine from his glass. It's like I'm watching everything in slow motion. A feeling of dread comes from out of nowhere and blindsides me.

"Kassidy, I met someone new. I think we should break up. I tried to see past all of this because you have such a pretty face." A feeling of anger rushes through me as Stanley waves his hands in the air. "You have potential if you lost some weight." He is acting like he just finished discussing the weather and it drives me nuts.

I look down at the plate of breadsticks sitting in the middle of us, contemplating why I had fallen for Stanley in the first place. I glance at the red tablecloth that lay neatly across the table but no answer forms to mind. Words flee my brain and all I want to do is ball my eyes out but I can't allow Stanley to see me cry. I can't give my now ex-boyfriend the satisfaction of winning. I glance at the two carat ring on my finger he just gave me the month before. I feel like my finger is suddenly on fire. I then take a deep breath before beginning to speak.

"I guess you want your engagement ring back, huh?"

"I think that would be best. Don't you? I can resell it to recoup my losses."

Hell, Stanley Jones is a cold piece of work. He is blunt about his intentions and doesn't give a damn who he hurts or how he hurts people, especially me, in the process

"What's her name?" I ask. I am a glutton for punishment.

"None of that matters now. The ring please," Stanley demanded as he held his hand out for the ring. His palm was facing upward and his fingers wiggled like a toddler who wants what everyone has instead of their own toys!

My lips begin to tremble and my insides start to

quiver like the beginning of an earthquake. I twist the ring off my finger and drop it into Stanley's upturned hand. I wonder what I ever found lovable in Stanley besides his dark chocolate skin, low cut fade, dark brown eyes, and thick kissable lips. He was a tall sexy cup of hot chocolate, and in this moment, I hate him.

"Thanks," he says as if he is making a money transaction. It makes sense considering he manages loans at the Trans-State Bank. I am a receptionist at the same bank and there is no way in hell I can work with Stanley now! I can't be in the same building as him. I am at risk of coming into contact with him day after day and that just isn't my cup of tea. My mind is made up! I will put in my two weeks notice of leave with Trans-State bank of Seattle as soon as possible

"Are you through eating?" he asks giving me a thorough glare of disgust.

I stare at him with mist in my eyes. I don't realize that I am midway through chomping on a breadstick I had picked up. Eating is almost like my own personal lifeline... I am such an emotional eater. I glance with envy around the restaurant at happy smiling couples dining in the intimate setting. Most whom are beautiful, slim women who are dining with their significant others.

"Stanley I can't believe that you would treat me like this. Have I ever meant anything to you? Anything at all?" I try to hold back my tears, but they slip treacherously from my eyes no matter how hard I try to blink them away.

"Kassidy, we haven't been working out for a long time. Maybe after you lose some weight we can try again. I do love you but— the sex is subpar at best between us these last few months."

"Stop lying, Stanley! You don't love me. I was plump when you met me. You said you liked women with meat on their bones. You said—,"

"Keep your damn voice under control. You don't want to bring unwanted attention to yourself. For your information, Kassidy, I said that two years ago when you were a size ten. You hooked me, and you just let yourself go. I warned you when I asked you to marry me last Christmas that you needed to get your eating habits under control. I will even buy you a membership at the Knight & Knight Brothers Workout Facility where I have a membership if you want me to."

"Fuck you, Stanley. I hope you and your new lover are as miserable as you've made me," I throw the breadstick I had been eating at him. It hits Stanley in the chest with a soft thump. I start to rise from my seat.

"Oh, that's very mature of you Kassidy. Why don't you act like a mature thirty two year old woman? Jessica is the epitome of a classy, beautiful young woman who has her shit together both physically and mentally. AND, she's only twenty two!"

"Did you just say Jessica?"

Suddenly Stanley goes rigid and silent.

"Are you talking about Jessica Chambers? The new intern from your loan department?"

"What if I am? Nothing will change things between us and we both know it."

"You're damn right about that. I never want to see your sorry ass again!" I spit out and brush tears of frustration from my face.

"I think that will be hard to do since we work together on a daily basis."

"We won't be working together for very long asshole. I haven't had a raise in God-knows-when anyway. It won't be no hardship for me to move on as soon as I have another job lined up." I say lashing out at him. I tug my dress down and smoothed the wrinkles from the clingy material. I had bought the dress especially for tonight. The sales clerk at Macy's had convinced me to buy the dress when I was admiring it on the sales rack last weekend. Now, I felt like I could have worn a sack and it still wouldn't have sufficed.

"Hey Kassidy," Stanley calls to me as I start to walk away.

"What?" I grunt as I half turn to face him. A hopeful breath catches in my chest. *Maybe he's having*

*a change of heart. Maybe he can love me uncondition-
ally after all.*

"Don't forget about my offer. I'll make that gym
membership happen for you. Just say the word."

My head whips around to face him so fast that my
neck makes a cracking sound. I march over to the table
and pick up my water glass and dump its contents over
his head. "You will not make me feel less than what I
really am. You are the one with the problem," I hiss.

Everyone in the restaurant looks our way. Whis-
pering voices and some chuckles can be heard. Some
are even pointing fingers our way. Stanley jumps up
from his seat huffing. I spot two servers and what
appears to be the manager heading our way.

"Damn you, Kassidy! You are a fucking bitch," he
shouts.

"That makes two of us!" I glare at him just as the
three employees are upon us.

"What seems to be the problem here? We can't
have—," the manager starts to say, but I cut him off.

"He's the problem but now he's someone else's
problem," I reply pointing at Stanley. A mortified look
crosses his face before I spin on my heels and flee the
building.

CHAPTER ONE

Dirk

I'm going over the Smidt contract and notice their numbers look off. This is a complete fuck up on their behalf that was completely avoidable if only they had taken the time to research all avenues and possibilities for the project. *Shit!* Fucking lazy employees who want to live in luxury but don't want to work their asses off for the money like they should. This shit won't fly if Smidt intends to continue doing business with N&D.

I'm already in a lousy mood because our assistant has decided she needs to spend more time with her husband and two kids. Haven't Nikolai and I been kind enough to her over the years? I guess not if she's going to treat us like this, especially when she takes days off work to care for her ill kids.

I vow the next person we hire will be single as fuck and free to put N&D first and foremost. I was sitting at my desk deep in thought when I get loudly interrupted by a knock at the door. "Enter," I direct.

Nola opens my office door with a file in hand. "Sit," I state with a nod of my head.

She takes a seat in one of the cushiony seats across from my desk.

"Dirk I'm sorry if you're disappointed in my decision—"

"Are those the latest projections from the last quarter?" I ask her putting the contract aside.

"Yes, sir."

"Good." I tap the desk with my finger for her to place the file on my desk. "Now, what were you saying about disappointing me?"

My assistant wrings her hands in her lap, momentarily seeming at a loss for words. "I'm sorry if it seems as if I'm abandoning the company. I just need to spend more time with my family. I won't apologize for that. I grew up in a household never seeing my parents. When they weren't working, they were traveling the world without my younger brother and I. I don't want that for my two girls, and my husband agrees. I've lined up someone with an impeccable background to interview for the job. I know you and Nikolai weren't thrilled by the previous candidates, but I assure you that you will like this one."

I know I've been an ass towards my assistant lately. The thing is, I'm not big on goodbyes, especially when it comes to a damn good employee. I take a deep breath and push my frustrations aside.

"Nola, you are invaluable to us. You will be missed. My annoyance with you leaving the company has been pure selfishness on my part, and that's putting it mildly." I pause and reach inside a drawer to pull out an envelope. "For your loyal service at N&D, I want you to have this. If we can do anything for you in the future, don't you dare hesitate to ask.

"You've done enough. I can't—"

"You can and you will." I stand, walk around the desk, and place the envelope in her hand. With trembling fingers, she opens it and looks inside.

"Oh my God! This is a certified check for two hundred fifty thousand dollars!" Nola stands with tears misting her eyes and throws her arms around me. "Thank you."

My frustrations have wholly dissipated. I guess I'm not a complete asshole after all.

"You deserve it," I reply, returning her embrace with a grin on my face.

Nikolai

"Thanks for handling business for me while I was out of the office. I know how much you hate saying goodbye," I say to Dirk.

I'm sitting at my desk, and Dirk is pacing the floor in front of me. I'm the voice of reason this time around it seems. I appear laid back when I'm anything but calm and full of composure.

"Dirk, we had to see this coming. Nola warned us how her husband Brad felt with her last pregnancy. I'm just surprised she didn't put in her resignation sooner."

Dirk stops pacing, leans down, and plants both hands across the desk.

"Fuck man. Don't you think I realize that? I'm a selfish prick- so sue me."

I chuckle at Dirk's foul mood. "Calm down man."

"I knew Nola's resignation was coming, but I don't want to go through another assistant. I don't give a single fuck about how great she is."

"Stop stressing out. I will personally handle the interview on tomorrow if you don't want to."

"Just make sure she's as proficient as, if not more so than, Nola.

"Look, Dirk, I get that Nola has been with us since

we started the business, but times have changed. It's normal that she needs to do what's best for herself and her family."

"Dammit, you're right," Dirk says. "I just have to accept it and move on, but fuck change all the same."

CHAPTER TWO

Kassidy

"Kassidy are you nervous about tomorrow?"

I wrinkle my nose and shrug my shoulders before sitting up straighter on the couch. I glance at my friend Anita. Anita is tall with a lithe like figure, short red hair, and a razor sharp tongue that can cut anyone down to size. I guess that's why we get along so well. I also have a low tolerance for bullshit.

Our appearance is as different as night and day. I'm short, measuring in at only five-feet, three-inches tall, with black hair styled in a chin-length bob, dark brown eyes, a size twelve at most, and smooth, warm, cinnamon-colored skin; whereas she is five-feet, nine-inches tall, with vivid red hair, blue eyes, a size two, and pale ivory skin. She is mostly cheerful with a positive outlook on life. Her pouty lips and sugary tone will turn sharp as a knife if someone gets on her bad side. However, she's a loyal friend and I love her like a sister.

"Um, to be honest, yes. I'm a thirty-two year old single woman going for an interview for a job with women who are at least ten years younger than me. Plus, I will be competing for the coveted assistant position at a renowned company. I just pray my skill set will nail me the job at N&D Inc."

Anita chuckles and takes a drink from her wine glass before speaking. "What? Are you seriously worried about not being able to compete with some twenty-two year old fresh out of college?"

"I am."

"Well, have you thought of doing more with your life than being someone's assistant Kass? You have so much potential. You could go back to college and finish that master's degree in business you're always talking about."

"Anita, do you know how many student loans I'm still paying for? I need this job; can you support me on this?"

Anita grins. "Of course I can support you. I'm your best friend, aren't I?"

"Of course you are, but I also know how opinionated you can be!"

"Would you have me any other way?" Anita replies with a great big sigh.

"You know damn well I wouldn't." I lean over and give her a reassuring pat on the arm.

"If you get the job, we will have to celebrate."

"Yes! That's an awesome plan!" I say to Anita with great hope that we will have something to celebrate.

CHAPTER THREE

Kassidy

THE NEXT MORNING

I'm nervous as hell about this interview. I give myself a quick glance in the mirror to see the image of a professional business woman in a two-piece conservative skirt and matching jacket looking back at me. I take big breaths knowing I need to get a move on if I want to make my appointment on time. I grab my handbag and keys and head out the door. Looking at my hooptie of a car, I moan in disgust.

"It's a steal," the salesman told me six months ago when I purchased it. It's a 2014 Honda Civic. I used my life savings of ten thousand dollars, plus I took out a loan to pay the rest of the twenty thousand dollars that

I owed. It was spotless, and it was my favorite color; a teal blue. It even came with upgraded leather seats and a sound system. It was a one owner car, and the old lady who had it before me really took remarkable care of it. The interior still smells new to this day. The salesman even showed me all the maintenance records and the car only had 40,000 miles on it.

Yeah, it's a real steal. *Not!* I got ripped off because now it's sounding like an old clunker. I purchased as is and now there's no way I can take it back.

I look over at my rundown, not-so-modern apartment building and swear to move in a swankier place if I get the new job. The faded moss-green paint on the walls has definitely seen better days. At least the neighbors are friendly. I wave at old Mrs. Lee when I see her peeping out her window. She waves back before letting her faded flower curtains fall back into place.

"Thank you, Jesus!" I say aloud when the engine finally fires up. I ease out my parking spot and reverse out onto the busy highway.

As I left my neighborhood, I navigate onto the interstate. This way will shorten my distance to N&D. I drive along the busy highway praying my car doesn't let me down along the way. The further I get into the city, the buildings become more frequent and the crowd of people denser.

I already know I need to turn right at the next stoplight. *I hate navigating around the city,* I think to myself. I start to weave my way down the street that will take me to the N&D building.

It's a forty-five minute commute from my neighborhood into the city of Seattle. I will never get use to the magnificence of this building. N&D Inc is extravagant, even on the outside. It's tall and the building towers above all the others. It has huge columns of concrete and is covered in glass. There's a sharp contrast to the city where N&D rests.

A silvery gray Mercedes S600 shoots past me to secure the parking spot I am about to enter. My middle finger is about to shoot up when I think better of it. I don't want to jeopardize my interview in case I run into the person again. The unsmiling woman slides out of her car, barely giving me a sneering glance.

I circle the parking deck once more. The parking decks are full of 2019 model cars. My mouth twists into a pout as I park my car between a BMW and a Lexus SUV. I switch off the ignition and hear another loud clunking sound. Damn, this car is a lemon for sure. I wonder how many people got a bad deal besides me, or am I the only fool that judged a used car by its appearance? I should have taken Anita's advice and test drove it to a reliable mechanic.

Getting out of my car, the morning air kisses against my cheeks. Seattle's busy traffic of blaring horns and fast paced business men and women causes my heart to pump. My heels click across the parking lot leading to the white marble of the large lobby. I move with a rhythm that keeps pace with my fast-paced heartbeat. The insides of my hands become sweaty. I dare not rub them on my skirt to leave a telling imprint of my nervousness on my clothes.

A security guard is the first person I encounter. I notice a man dressed in all black at the front of the main entrance near the elevator that the email said I was destined to get on. His name-tag reads 'Branson'.

The size of his bulky body makes me gulp and I notice a gun is strapped to his side. Anyone with any common sense, which nowadays is almost nobody, wouldn't dare to try anything with this man on guard.

"Name and ID please." His black eyes clash with my brown ones. Branson's skin is darkly tanned. I become disarmed when his stern face suddenly flashes a white smile.

"Erm, my name is Kassidy Davis and I'm here for an interview for the assistant's position for Mister Pierce and Mister Hawkings," I reply sliding my ID across the security counter. My nervousness only increases after the guard gives me a visitors pass and I stroll to the elevator. I breathe deeply to try and calm my nerves. I want this job in a bad way. I need it to better my circumstances in life. I know deep down I have to try even if I fail. At least I won't have to see that asshole Stanley's face day in and day out. *Good riddance to him!*

I don't know how or why I stupidly fell in love with a buffoon like him. I will not give in and say it's my fault he did what he did. The things he did are on him and him alone. I'd much rather be by myself and without a man, than to be tied to a man who didn't respect and love me unconditionally.

I need to focus and get on my game face for the assistant's job I'm interviewing for. I *cannot* mess this up.

Continuing my inner pep talk, my breath catches in my throat when I step onto the elevator. I send up a quick prayer that I will get the job. The elevator made a ping and the doors began to open. I step out at the smoky-glass entrance that houses N&D's executive offices. I notice right away the company's name is emblazoned in golden metallic writing across the double doors. I'm feeling overwhelmed as I stare at the array of professionally dressed young women sitting around the waiting area. I suddenly feel like I really need to go shopping. Maybe Anita and my other friends can get together for a shopping expedition at our local thrift store soon.

I take in another deep breath. I check in with the

receptionist, a nicely dressed white woman with a friendly smile plastered to her face.

My skin flushes against my dark tone as I make my way to the receptionist's desk. "Hi my name is Kassidy Davis, and I'm here for the interview.

"Hi Kassidy, welcome to N&D. Let me check to see who I need to direct you to." The receptionist taps her keys over the keyboard before she speaks again. "Oh yes, you're supposed to see Nola, the administrative assistant to Nikolai and Dirk. Go down the hall to your right, and her office is the first one on the left," she directs me. "Good luck," the receptionist adds.

CHAPTER FOUR

Kassidy

The tapping sounds of my heels drumming against the marbled flooring accompanies me as I walked off the elevator toward the assistant's desk. I notice the walls are covered with brown and beige toned paint and beautiful artwork hangs from the walls. There are two large sections of offices across from each other and between them a smaller cubicle where a pleasant faced woman stand up to greet me. I feel a wave of nervousness hit me in the pit of my belly.

"Hello welcome to the offices of N&D Incorporated. My name is Nola." The woman with short brown hair and somewhat thin lips greets me with a welcoming smile. Nola extend her hand toward me. "And you are?"

"Hi Nola, my name is Kassidy Davis." I extend my hand to shake her hand. "I'm here for the assistant job. I have an interview.

"Of course Ms. Davis. Have a seat," she extends her arm towards a comfortable looking waiting area. "There is an applicant with the boss at the moment, and another to be seen before you but she hasn't arrived yet. You will be seen as soon as the boss finishes up with her," Nola informs me.

"Call me Kassidy please," I reply.

"Very well Kassidy. Would you like a coffee, tea, or water while you wait in the waiting room over there?" I look over to see a glass door that leads to a waiting room in the direction she's pointing.

"No thank you," I reply. I walk the short distance to the waiting area and take a seat. I breathe heavily as I try and expel my nervousness, but nothing seems to work.

I sit in silence on the sofa in the seating area, studying the various artwork hanging on the walls. I take in a large abstract painting with wild, vivid colors which is on display. It is almost like a child went wild slinging paint onto a canvas. I bet an enormous fee was charged for a painting like that.

A young woman that looks to be fresh out of college walks into the sitting room and takes a seat in alignment to me. Her bright blue eyes meet mine, and she gives me a tight smile. I nod a greeting and smile back.

Soon, the lady gets up to look at the different paintings on the walls. Suddenly, she turns towards me to speak. "Hello, my name is Crystal. And you are?" Her brow arches inquiringly.

"I'm Kassidy."

Crystal asks, "Are you here for the interview too?"

"Yes, I am."

Crystal's mouth sets into a thin smile. "Good luck," she says as if I'm going to need it and retakes her seat.

"Thanks," I add. I don't dare lie and wish her good luck because, in reality, I want this job in a bad way. No need for me to tell her something I don't mean.

"Miss Crystal Korbin, you can come with me," Nola enters the room cutting off all other conversation between us.

Crystal rises from her seat and slings her silky golden hair over her shoulder. She pauses in the doorway, looks back at me, and gives me a beauty queen wave—all fingers. I frown because I know a catty move when I see it. So high schoolish. I'm a mature woman and don't have the time for such games. I hope there aren't many people like her that work here or will be working here. If so, they would soon know that I don't have time for bullshit.

CHAPTER FIVE

Nikolai

"Right this way, Miss Davis. Nikolai Pierce is ready to see you now," the secretary walks me to another office.

"Miss Davis," inquires a deep and inquisitive voice.

I straightened my spine as I confronted one of the owners of N&D for the first time. The office is massive. *Oh my God! He is absolutely gorgeous!* The black and gold plaque on the door states the office belongs to Nikolai Pierce. I hope my rapid beating heart doesn't let on how nervous I am. His silvery gaze pierces straight through me. My legs become weak, and I fight to stay standing on my feet. The business magazines didn't do justice to this gorgeous and chiseled man that stands before me.

29

Mr. Pierce is young, vibrant and broad-shouldered. His golden-blond hair is worn slicked back, and he looks like a wet fantasy waiting to happen. His aroma cloaks me, and he smells a bit like sage, with a hint of vanilla. *Delicious!*

I give myself a mental shake and clear my throat before I speak. "Yes, I'm Kassidy Davis." I blink rapidly and look somewhere over his right shoulder to avoid his piercing stare. I notice an arch to his sexy lips. I wonder if at that moment he can tell how flustered I am. His eyes seem to know something that I don't in the way his glance peruses me from my head down to my four-inch heels. Suddenly, he grabs me by surprise and extends his hand. I place my hand inside his to shake. When I go to pull away, he holds on with that one-sided smile still attached to his lips.

Nikolai's stare holds mine in a fiery glance. Mr. Pierce is tall, at least six-foot-three inches in height. I have to tilt my neck to look up at him. I continue to blink in rapid succession as his eyes burn deep into my brown orbs. The depth of his stare touches me to my very soul. I can feel color rising to my brown skin. I hope to God I'm dark enough to hide my flustering emotions.

Finally, Nikolai releases my hand, but only to place his at the small of my back. I shiver instantly from the pressure of his warm hand. *I am too old for this! How can a younger man affect me in this way?*

"Come and take a seat," Nikolai directs me. "Please make yourself comfortable," Nikolai adds. Nikolai's eyes are like ice, but every time he looks at me I get hot all over. *How the hell can I work in this state day in and day out?* I never once felt this way around Stanley. *My God, this man is too sexy for his own good,* I thought. I know that I need to remain professional. After all, Mr. Nikolai Pierce could be my potential boss.

"Thank you," I reply sitting back in the soft cushioned leather seat. I once again attempt to tear my gaze away. I take the time to breathe in deeply before slowly exhaling. I glance around the sizeable pristine office while trying to get my emotions under control.

I think to myself that my new boss, Nikolai Pierce, is going to be hard to work around without getting hot and bothered. I have an inkling feeling that if I don't keep my head on straight, I will be fighting a losing battle where my head and heart are concerned.

"Are you husband or boyfriend free?" Nikolai catches me off center with his words.

I think about my recent breakup with that cheater Stanley. "Um, pardon me? Is that a requirement for me to get the job?" I ask a question of my own. I am still upset about Stanley dumping me. It is such an embarrassment, and it does absolutely nothing for my self-esteem. Stanley would never know the depth of hurt this break up has caused me. Also, I know the demographics of black women in America. Demographically speaking, only twenty-nine percent of black women are married compared to forty-eight percent of all Americans. And only fifty percent of black women like me have never been married compared to thirty-three percent of all Americans. I bristle under Nikolai's bold stare.

"No, Kassidy, that isn't a requirement."

"Are you stereotyping me because I'm a black woman?" I can feel the beginnings of a frown starting on my face.

So, that's how young rich, handsome billionaire bosses like Nikolai Pierce keep their company thriving with a specific type. Why did I think N&D would seriously hire someone like me? I am assured that I am more than qualified for this position, and I know it. Let's see what drivel he comes up with to deny me the job.

"To be honest Kassidy, I asked that question for personal reasons." His gray gaze strokes my body as if he's physically touching me with his hands.

My body begins to tremble. My mouth opens to speak but closes before any words come out. I snap my mouth shut because I don't want to look like a gaping fish.

Suddenly he disarms me with another sexy ass grin and my frown completely dissipates. My lips automatically turn up into a returning smile as I look at Nikolai; I silently pray he will be my new boss. This interview is going far from how I imagined.

I dispel a long breath. "To be truthful, my boyfriend dumped me for a younger and thinner woman. According to him, my weight is getting out of control," as the truth divulges from my mouth, I can't help but break eye contact.

"Ahem, well I say your ex is a damn fool. Don't you dare change a hair on your head. You are a beautiful woman Kassidy Davis, and I'm sure any real man will be happy if you were his. Your lovely curves and all. Besides, you are definitely not fat. The asshat must be blind."

My body warms all over because of his words. "Thank you, Nikolai," I say as my smile grows wider.

"I am only speaking the truth." There he goes again with his penetrating stare, making me feel all hot and bothered. I bet all the women feel like this in his presence. A woman has to be dead not to feel anything when Nikolai gives them his undivided attention.

My heart rate increases sitting here under Nikolai's desirous scrutiny, I become slicker in my nether regions. I squeeze my thighs together and bite my bottom lip to staunch a moan from slipping past my lips.

What the hell is wrong with me? I have never felt this way before. I feel embarrassed to be sitting here like a woman in heat. One more squeeze of my thighs will be all it takes and I will cum.

"Are you alright Kassidy? Do you need some ice water or anything?" Nikolai asks me with an all-knowing glint in his gaze.

"Um, no. I'm fine," I lie.

"That you are." His silvery gaze roams over me again. My eyes close on their own volition as my thighs press together against my will. I grab the armrest of the chair and squeeze as electrical shocks run rapidly inside my core.

~

NIKOLAI

"Fuck!" Nikolai's voice growls out. My eyes fly open, and our eyes clash. "Damn, I can use a strong drink," he says raking a hand through his silken strands. I sit there totally humiliated. I feel like bolting for the door and never looking back, but I sit there like a statue to see if Nikolai will bring my humiliation to light.

"Shall we continue with the interview?" he asks.

I can only nod and attempt a smile as though nothing has happened. "Tell me about yourself," Nikolai says as he sits behind his desk. He doesn't waste any time with his questions.

"Well, I served as a receptionist for the past ten years at my former job. I do have references included with the application I filled out online for this job. During my time at my previous employment, I have been commended on my customer service skills, my ability to work with others, and my commitment to the company. I hardly took any time off unless it was absolutely necessary."

"What makes you unique?"

"My uniqueness is my ten years of experience on the job. Don't take this the wrong way, but I notice this is a company that consists of twenty-something-year-olds. I'm thirty-two and may seem over the hill compared to most of the young people here, but let me assure you, in most cases, experience triumphs youth. I know what it takes to create positive energy in the workplace."

"Why do you want to work here?"

"I must admit that I've read several articles about this company. I read that you and your partner are lifelong friends who went to college together and started this multi-billion dollar company. I am intrigued, and I admire the business acumen you two acquired at such a young age. I also admire your company's mission to help graduate students in need of jobs. I know what college loans do to a person. I'm still paying them to this day. I applaud your company on the diversity of your hiring practices as well. Also, your company is in the top ten in all the business magazines in the U.S. and abroad."

Nikolai nods, and a grin spreads across his handsome face. I can tell he's very proud of his accomplishments. Who wouldn't be?

"It seems you've done your homework, Kassidy. Tell me, what motivates you and what are you passionate about?"

"I want to feel a part of something greater. At night when I lie down, I want to feel as if I've accomplished making a difference in the company I'm working for. Of course, paying my bills and putting food on the table motivates me. But it's more than that."

"I get that. Great answer. Why are you leaving your current job?

"I'm not going anywhere; I haven't had a promotion and only two raises in the ten years I've worked there. Simply put, it's time for me to move on."

"Are you willing to work extra hours, or travel when necessary?

"Yes, I'm not afraid of hard work. I am also free to

travel. I have only me to worry about, and nothing is holding me back."

"Excellent! Why should N&D hire you?"

"My highest value to any company is my ability to work independently, freeing up time for my employers to focus on the needs of their business. You tell me what to do, and I will get it done." I don't believe how easy it is to answer these questions. It seems as if my uneasiness dissipated by the warmth of Nikolai's voice.

"Kassidy, the job is yours if you want it."

I have to fight myself to keep my mouth from dropping open. *Oh my God!* Just like that, the job is mine. I wanted it, but I can't believe it. "Yes! I want the job. Thank you, Nikola. Thank you so much."

"You will need to meet with my partner Dirk Hawkings. A fair word of warning—Dirk is still coming to grips with Nola's decision to leave. Don't let his grumpy attitude dissuade you in any way. I'm sure he will want to welcome you on board anyway."

My heart plummets and a butterfly like feeling settles in the pit of my belly. *What if Nikolai's partner doesn't want to hire me? What then?*

Nikolai

I watch Kassidy through hooded lids.

"Fuck!" I growl when a hint of her arousal fumes in the air.

Fuckkk!

I suppress another deep growl and sniff the air; I can smell Kassidy's arousal. My dick lengthens, but I stop myself from taking her. Here and now, I want to fuck her so deep until she can't walk straight. A sexual, predatory feeling courses through my body. The look on Kassidy's face and the desire in her eyes makes me ache with fierce lust.

The growing throb in my cock intensifies when she licks her plump lips. The beast inside claws and scrapes to come out and play.

She looks nervous all of a sudden, and I don't want to scare her away.

This woman seduces me without even knowing what she does to me. Her body calls to me, unlike any woman has before. Kassidy is not only beautiful and luscious with curves upon curves, but she's sweet and full of intelligence. That within itself turns me on.

Her thick, dark hair make me want to sift my fingers through it. The simmering heat in the depths of her brown eyes make me want to lose myself in their luminosity. The darkness of her skin glows and makes me want to lick every inch of her. I allow my gaze to shift to her legs. My nostrils flare as I think of her thighs splayed over my shoulders with my face buried against her mound.

The craving for chocolate... Kassidy's kind of chocolate, is overwhelming. I want to strip her bare, take her bountiful breasts in my hand, before taking her nipples into my mouth.

I continue to watch her lovely face. Her eyes dilate, and I crave to be lodged deep in her wetness. I can imagine her pussy squeezing my shaft tight.

My blood is pumping through my veins, hot with need.

I'm a blazing inferno inside as an insatiable need licks up my spine and blazes its way straight to my shaft. Kassidy is all I see. I want her wrapped around me, balls deep, and my mouth claiming every fucking inch of her.

The need inside me is on an all-time high since Kassidy walked into this building. I know Dirk feels it too, no matter how gruff his manners are towards Kassidy, but that's just Dirk's personality. His growl is much worse than his bite. *Although the need to bite Kassidy right now is its own form of torture.*

Why the hell did she have to be so fucking desirable?

Sexual frustration continues to penetrate deep within, making my muscles tense. I clench my jawline and grind my teeth to keep from pouncing on Kassidy and scaring her away.

The predator in me wants to take and claim her this instant. I clench my fists by my sides, pushing down the idea of following through with my burning desires.

Today isn't the day to hunt and conquer. My animalistic nature would have to wait to satisfy its lust. My beast inwardly howls at my restraint.

My beast snarls. *Take her now.... mine!*

Ours! Another voice growls inside my head.

Ours, I agree and exhale.

I push back the force inside me once again that wants out. *Soon,* Kassidy Davis will be mine.

"Ahem," Kassidy clears her throat bringing me out of my desirable thoughts.

"Dirk's office is the one across from this one. I'll let him know you're on your way over. I'm looking forward to working closely with you, Kassidy," I say standing to my feet. I watch Kassidy rise to her feet at my words.

I stroll over and reach for both of her hands; my eyes plunge down into hers. I notice a visible shudder run through her body from my intense gaze. My lip arches up on one side and I want to kiss her. *Damn it, I want to fuck her.*

"I'm looking forward to working with you Kassidy," I barely get out. I inhale her sweet scent and warmth settles into a part of my body that causes havoc on my senses. I grow harder.

I gather my control and say, "I'll see you to the door."

"Thank you," Kassidy replies before stepping out the door to make her way across the hall. She looks back and catches my eyes glued to her rounded ass. I grin, as she turns back from my forceful gaze.

The urge to take her pumps continuously through my veins.

Dirk

Nikolai just sent me a text saying he is impressed with Kassidy's professional demeanor. Even though she appeared to be ill-at-ease during the interview, she was well spoken and held up. *She's the one!* He ends the text and I put my phone away just as I call for her to enter my office.

I take notice that Kassidy is beautiful. I can't help myself from taking in her flawless dark skin and the impeccable way her two piece skirt suit fit her like a second skin. I lick my lips as my eyes roam over her busty cleavage. Only two buttons are left undone, but

the softness of her breasts penetrate through my imag-
ination.

I only ask her a few questions and I notice just
before each question she pauses and angles her head to
one side to expose her delicate neckline. I wonder what
her skin would feel like against my lips.

Kassidy's hair is chin length and styled in a bob
that bounces slightly when she turns her head. I can
find myself drowning in the depths of her chocolate
dark eyes when our gazes clash.

My eyes land on the fullness of her lips. She wears
a nude gloss which give them a plush look; undoubtedly meant to be kissed and fucked by my cock.

Shit! What am I thinking? I pull my pants leg down
to make room for my growing erection. This interview
is going much different than any I've given all because
of the dark beauty sitting before me.

My eyes drip over her body even though I try not
to. Kassidy's womanly curves call out to me. My body
tenses. My heart thunders a little faster, pumping
blood like fuel through my veins. My jaw clenches and
my cock swells eagerly against my dress slacks.

It's been too fucking long since I've felt instanta-
neous lust for a woman. This just won't do.

I can see why Nikolai sent me the text filled with
excitement. We're similar, my best friend and I, when
it comes to our type in women. Business is another

matter where Nikolai and I click so well together. We are both courageous; driven hard to prosper and we leave no stone unturned until we get the job done.

Shit, I can't explain the feeling that's come over me since Kassidy entered this office. I want to be wary of her. I want to tell her she's not hired, but I can't find any logical reason to do so. I know this woman will be trouble. I can't explain how but I just know. Some things are just a known fact, as is this sudden obsession to see her naked and lying beneath my body while I thrust my shaft inside her slick cunt to the hilt. Fiery lust emblazons me, and I clench my jaw to stop these fucking emotions from zooming through my body.

Thoughts from a past I don't like to think about flit through my mind.

This beautiful woman before me wreaks havoc on my libido. My instincts tell me to claim her, but my head goes against what my inner beast is craving.

I'm flawed. I don't know how to do romantic relationships. Love and life are fleeting at best. That was proven to me long ago when my mother walked away from me. I was only four years old.

I often wondered why she didn't love me enough to keep me. Then one day, when I was around nine years old, I heard the uncle who grudgingly took me in tell his girlfriend that my mom was raped late one night as she walked home from work. He said she didn't have the heart to abort me, but she didn't have the heart to keep me either.

My years have been marred with pain, hurt, and the absence of love. I had no intention of ever risking love, suffering, and above all else, *loss*. So, I closed my heart off, I played the field with women without letting anyone get close, or me giving away anything more than my body. I hurt some of those women along the way. I never needed anything serious; I always remained detached. Yet now all of that self-preservation seemed to go up in smoke when Kassidy walked into my life.

Being around Kassidy causes me to wrestle with the prospect of intimacy *and* allowing her into my heart. I knew that I hadn't dealt with the pain of my past; that I didn't want to reopen my heart. Although the beast in me demanded that I do just that. Over time, I grew numb to my actions and the thoughtlessness of them.

I was a loner with a big chip on my shoulder growing up until I met Nikolai. Once I did, we became inseparable. He became my brother. My family. My business partner. *Still,* I have this feeling that every woman was like my mother. That thought lived in this tiny bubble in my brain and caused me to distrust women.

. . .

Though the thought of loving a woman like my mother caused me pain, the beast inside me snaps and snarls for me to lay claim on Kassidy.

The last thing I ever thought I'd need, especially at this time with my fucked up way of thinking, was a woman to walk into my life and disrupt my lifestyle.

I learned long ago that fierce lust soon fizzles out once I've fucked my goal. I push myself to end this interview as quickly as possible. I need to get my head straight. I snap out my questions like bullets. I realize I'm curt, but I can't help it.

Perhaps it's the way her nipples press hard against her clingy shirt, and the way her luscious brown cleavage calls for me to bury my face between her globes. I wonder what kind of panties she has on under that tight skirt of hers.

When the interview is over, I stand from my seat and extend my hand out for Kassidy to shake. When she grabs my hand, I can feel an electrified zing run through my system.

Why is this woman having this effect on me? I attempt to shake it off. *Fuck.* This woman is made to love and fuck. *Oh hell, where did that thought come from?*

Damn it. I want to fuck our new assistant, and it makes me all kinds of angry.

Kassidy

From the moment that I raised a hand to knock on the dark mahogany door with a gold emblazoned plaque naming the office as Dirk Hawkings', I gasped aloud when the door is abruptly opened before my hand even made contact.

Dirk stood before me, slightly shorter than his partner. He is about six-feet-one-inch tall, and a little less broad with a sharp jawline and brilliant blue eyes. His hair was long and black, pulled back in a loose ponytail. He's dressed more relaxed in gray slacks and a white dress shirt with the top three buttons undone.

"Miss Davis, come in. I'm sure you know I'm Dirk Hawkings, Co-CEO of N&D Incorporated. You may call me Mr. Hawkings. Have a seat and let's get down to business, shall we?"

"Oh, okay," I walk over to the chair he indicates for me to sit in. "It's a pleasure to—"

Mr. Hawkings cuts me off. He's a rude one, but I sit stiffly and attempt to hold my smile in place.

"Let me explain that our assistant, Nola McAllister, is leaving to spend more time with her husband and kids. The person we hire needs to be at our beck and call," he says in a gruff tone, border lining on unfriendly. "Do you have any problems with that, Miss Davis?" His icy blue eyes pierce me to the bone.

I almost become speechless, but I mutter through by saying, "Mr. Hawkings, I can assure you that my credentials are in order, to do this job. I—"

"Less talk Miss Davis and more action. Can you start work tomorrow morning?"

"Yes, I can."

"Good. You may see your way out and report to me first thing tomorrow morning." He gave me a dismissive stare before swiveling his chair around to face the picturesque window.

My nails bit into the palm of my hand from clenching my fist too tight. I grit my teeth from an effort to remain quiet. If I didn't need this job, I would tell Mr. Hawkings where to shove it. Instead, I stood without a word and headed out the door.

As I leave the office, I force myself to not look back at him. I can feel his stare burning into my back. *What's wrong with me? Why am I letting these men get under my skin like this?* I close the door and walk to the elevator. I'm hoping it will open as fast as possible so I can get out of here and regain control.

My heart wants to beat out of my chest. Finally, the elevator door slides open. As I step inside, it cloaks me within its metal space. My hands cover my face. My mind screams as I punch the button to the first floor. Once the elevator stops and the doors slide open, I dash out of the building and to the safety of my car like my life depends on it. I attempt to get my breathing under control before I start the ignition. Thank God my car doesn't give me any trouble because Dirk Hawkings just caused my day to go to shit.

CHAPTER SIX

Kassidy

I've been working at N&D for an entire week and Mr. Hawkings' demeanor towards me hasn't changed much. On several occasions I have caught him staring those dark blue eyes my way. Mr. Hawkings' stare is enough to set me on the edge of my seat. Like now, he walks into my office, his piercing eyes are locked on mine. My breath lodges in my chest causing goosebumps to cover my skin. *Why can't I look away?* He's mean and I dislike him. He's nothing like the friendly, warm-hearted Nikolai who oozes calmness. Mr. Hawkings' eyes drag slowly over my body. I berate myself silently for letting him have this effect on me. He's only twenty-seven and I should not be thinking he's sexy. But I do. Shame on me.

"Miss Davis, will you be finished with the Schultz report anytime soon?" His voice penetrates my thoughts and makes me focus back on business.

"I'm on it, Mr. Hawkings. I will have the report finished before I leave the office."

Dirk Hawkings arches a brow. "Good. Leave the report on my desk if I'm not in my office. I have a meeting that may run late."

"Of course, sir."

My boss stares at me. I shiver from the deliberate look in his blue eyes. Suddenly, he nods and turns to leave. I am still sitting there feeling hot and flustered with my mouth slightly open.

I take a small drink from the bottle of water on my desk and get back to work. About an hour later, there is a light tapping sound at my door.

"Come in," I call out.

The office door opens, and Cecelia, one of the many secretaries at N&D, walks in. She closes the door behind her. "Hey, do you want to get lunch? A few coworkers and I are going to a restaurant not too far from here. The day is beautiful out, and we can walk."

I give Cecelia a friendly smile. Ever since I started working here, she's made me feel welcome. I give her a nod just as my belly boldly rumbles.

"Well, looks like someone is hungry."

I shrug and laugh. "It seems so. I didn't get to eat much of a breakfast this morning."

"Okay, grab your purse and let's go," Cecelia replies.

We made it to the restaurant ten minutes later. Cecelia's friends are already seated at a table for four.

"Great! You two made it," a guy with brown hair and dimples says once Cecelia and I are seated.

"Kassidy, I'm not sure if you've met Pete Abrams, and this is Allie Meyers from the sales department," Cecelia explains as she introduces me to the blonde haired woman sitting beside Pete.

I notice right off that Allie isn't near as friendly as Pete. Her sour mood isn't going to stop me from enjoying my lunch hour though. *I'm starving!*

"How are you enjoying working for our two sexy-as-sin bosses?" Cecelia asks me once we've placed our orders and the food arrives.

"So far so good. I'm still finding my way around the office and building. I do know they both expect excellency and I give them my best."

"That job should have been mine," Allie blurts out.

My eyes widen as I assess the look on Allie's face. Her green eyes narrow on me as I stuff a roll into my mouth. "I'm sorry," I reply not knowing what else to say.

"Well Kassidy, have you lived in the Seattle area all your life?" Pete asks trying to change the subject.

"Yes, I'm Seattle born and bred, although my parents have settled in Tampa, Florida since they retired two years ago."

"Oh, that's nice. So are you married?" Allie inquires.

"No."

"Do you have a boyfriend?" Allie asks.

"I'm afraid not. Are you married, Allie?"

"No, but I have my eyes on a certain someone at the office," she admits.

"Who? Is it Nikolai, or Dirk?" Cecelia asks.

"Maybe it's both," Allie giggles. The fine hairs at the back of my neck stick out. There is something about her laugh that is grating on my last nerves. The thought of Allie being with either Nikolai or Dirk doesn't settle too well within my spirit.

I smile and finish eating as my coworkers continue to chat. Every time my glance lands on Allie, she shoots me a dirty look. *What the hell is her problem?* I think to myself. Whatever Allie's problem is, she needs to keep it to her damn self.

I exhale in a sigh of relief once my lunch hour is up and I'm sitting back at my desk.

"Kassidy." A thick, gruff baritone voice rumbles out

my name, and a tremble courses its way through my body. My eyes slide up from the computer, and my heart accelerates in my chest.

My other boss, Nikolai Pierce, has entered my office without so much as a knock. His silver colored eyes plunge into mine, making my panties instantly saturate with my wetness. There is something animalistic about my two bosses. I can't pinpoint exactly why they give off that vibe.

He's looking damn fine in a dark Tom Ford vest, and a custom-made light blue shirt with his sleeves rolled back halfway up his muscular forearms. His chiseled jawline looks strong, his lips kissable; his simmering gaze seems to sizzle right through me.

"Um, sir, is there something I can help you with?" *Why the hell is my thirty-two, soon to be thirty three-year-old ass getting all hot and bothered by my younger bosses? This just won't do!* I try to calm myself down but the succession rate is in the negative.

"I want to talk with you, but not here. Will you follow me?"

Shit! What did I do? I hope I wasn't in any kind of trouble. "Yes sir," I reply standing, grabbing a pen and notepad in case I need to take notes.

I tremble as I follow behind Nikolai to his plush office. The room is enormous with white walls, large windows and a perfect view of the landscape below. He walks straight to his desk and takes a seat. He gives me a smothering glance from the top of my head to my feet before he speaks.

There will be no repeat of me cumming just from being in his presence— I silently reprimand myself.

"Take a seat." The sensuousness of his voice resonates through me. I walk on jittery legs to take the seat in front of his desk.

I can feel a trickle of sweat slide down between the plump mounds of my breast. I shiver as my brown eyes connect with Nikolai's. My body warms all over, and I can feel my slick core clench as I lick my lips. My boss' eyes follow the swipe of my tongue.

"Ahem," I clear my throat, cross my legs and squeeze them together to staunch the flow of my desire. "Mr. Pierce, can I ask why you need to—"

"In due time, Miss Davis." Nikolai grunts and his gray eyes never leave mine. I nervously nibble on my bottom lip.

"Okay," I nod as I become lost for words.

"How do you like working here so far, Miss. Davis?" he growls deep in his throat. Slowly, he gets up, makes his way to the front of his desk and sits on the edge. I can't help but notice the huge bulge in his slacks. "Do you see something you like, Miss Davis?"

"Um, I beg your pardon?" I stutter out, gasping as he stares at me.

Whew! It's getting hotter in here. I wonder if I am starting to get hot flashes.

"No, I will not pardon you," Nikolai replies.

I gasp in surprise when I see the grin on his face and the twinkle in his eyes. *Shit!* He's teasing me while I sit here getting all hot and bothered.

I clear my throat again and speak in my most professional tone to answer his earlier question, "I do like working here. I have passed this building and wished to someday work here for many years. I'm thankful my wish came true. I appreciate you hiring me and I'm aware that you could have chosen someone much younger perhaps."

Nikolai's brow creases as his stare settles on my lips again. My tongue reflexively swipes against my bottom lip again. He stands and walks over to me. Nikolai leans down and places a hand on either side of my chair, imprisoning me. I can feel his minty breath caressing my lips. He makes me shiver being this close to him. I could inhale his intoxicating scent, and I jump when Nikolai speaks near my ear. His words are hot and seductive. "Do you know how beautiful you really are?"

I give my head a negative shake as I am too afraid

to verbally speak. *Am I dreaming?* I can't believe this is happening. *Is my boss really coming on to me?* My pussy once again begin to leak in Nikolai's presence. The office door opens; I gasp and pull away from Nikolai's lustful gaze.

"Fuck," he grumbles just before the office door opens and enters my other boss Dirk Hawkings. Nikolai stands to his full height and stalks back to his desk. I can't help but delight in seeing the massive erection beneath his slacks before he takes a seat, even if I am embarrassed to be caught in this position.

"The Briscoe account is trying to cause us some trouble," Dirk walks into Nikolai's office without knocking. Thank God he came when he did to stop me from making a simpering fool of myself.

"You ever heard of knocking?" Nikolai looks at me and winks before turning his eyes back to his partner.

"Why do I have to knock? Was I interrupting something?" The words growl from Dirk's lips, as he turns to me with a scowl on his handsome face.

I know I'm a new employee here but I'm getting tired of his attitude. I've been nothing but professional and do every assignment he and Nikolai give me to the letter. I even worked extra hours this week without a grumble. I come in early to make sure I have my work done on time. Why does he hate me? I wonder if it's because I'm black...

"Cool it Dirk. Kassidy and I were just going over a file. What's going on with the Briscoe account?"

"Man, Briscoe is a fucking idiot. He wants to change the terms of our agreement now since he's ready to sign. We are giving him far beyond the market value for the property in Texas as it is."

"I agree but getting hot headed isn't going to help matters. Let me call him, set up a lunch meeting with him and I'll get to the bottom of his problem." Nikolai's voice is calm and reasoning as he talks to Dirk.

"Have at it, the fucking good that will do," Dirk replies.

Dirk rakes his hand through his silky, long, black hair. He turns to me and I flush when he catches me staring at him. His eyes narrows and travel to my thighs when I nervously cross and uncross them again.

I feel a tingling up my spine as Dirk's eyes land back on mine. "Well Nikolai, if you're through with me, I'll go back to my office to let the two of you talk."

"No. Stay. I'm far from through with you," Nikolai's smooth voice makes me shiver.

"Why do you call him Nikolai and call me Mr. Hawkings?" Dirk's sneering voice brings my attention back to him.

I frown before replying, "Because you directed me to, Mr. Hawkings."

"I'm now directing you to call me Dirk. Do you

have a problem with that, Kassidy?" He grunts, emphasizing my first name.

"No sir, I have no problem with that whatsoever, Dirk."

Nikolai clasps his hands together. "We do pride ourselves on being informal around here. Now that that's settled, Kassidy you can come with me to lunch."

"It's not lunch time Nikolai and we still have business to discuss. There is no time to be fucking around—"

"It's the perfect time to be fucking around as you so crudely put it," Nikolai's voice is cheery. He rises from his seat and walks around from his desk to take me by the arm, pulling me to my feet. "I'm taking my hard working assistant to lunch. I'll see you when I get back," Nikolai adds with a smirky grin on his face.

Nikolai

I place my hand at the small of Kassidy's back and lead her in the restaurant. "I called in a reservation earlier. Nikolai Pierce," I tell the hostess once we arrive at the hostess stand.

"Of course," the hostess signals for a waiter. "Table of two for Mr. Pierce," she tells the waiter.

We follow the waiter after he grabs two menus and lead us to an intimate table for two that is situated by a window facing a beautiful view of the ocean.

"Are you ready to order?" the waiter asks once we are seated.

"Kassidy?" I question her studying the menu the waiter placed before us.

"I think I'll have the cob salad and a lemonade to drink," she didn't waste any time perusing the menu.

"I'll have the grilled halibut, seasoned potatoes, and mixed vegetables," I tell the waiter.

"What to drink?"

"I will have a lemonade also," I add as the waiter gathers the menus.

"Very good. I will bring your drinks out shortly. Your meals should arrive in about ten minutes." I thank the waiter and he walks off.

Shortly our drinks are placed before us.

"Mm, this is good," Kassidy takes a sip of her lemonade. She licks her plump lip to capture a bead of lemonade on her bottom lip.

My cock hardens instantly. It craves to be the one that Kassidy licks— I crave to have her mouth wrapped around my erection and pumping it down her throat.

"What? Do I have something on my mouth or something?"

My eyes jerk up to her brown orbs. An easy grin flits across my lips. "No, I was just thinking—"

Our food arrives. I'm thankful I don't have to fib. Kassidy seems to let the question drop as she glances at her well-constructed salad. The salad looks delicious with their knobs of cheese, jutting cucumbers and little slivers of steaming grilled chicken.

"The salad looks almost too pretty to eat doesn't it?" asks Kassidy. She forks some in her mouth and before I can stop myself a groan escapes.

Kassidy's eyes widen and her clash with mine. I feel as if I've jumped into crashing waves, the impact this woman has on me is sensually electrifying.

We continue staring into each other's eyes. I imagine how hot her pussy would feel wrapped around my cock.

"Hello Nikolai, I thought that was you." A woman's voice bursts through the sensual haze between Kassidy and me. A frown because of the interruption appears between my brows.

"Ah, Aimee, hello." I find it hard to tear my gaze away from my beautiful assistant.

What are the possibilities that I would run into a fuck buddy that I had just fucked the night before?

"Who is this?" Aimee's blue eyes land on Kassidy. My assistant places her fork down and dabs at her fuckable mouth with a linen napkin.

"This is my new assistant Kassidy. Kassidy this is my friend Aimee."

"Oh, so that's what you are calling me now. That's not what you called me last—"

"Um, excuse me, I need to use the ladies room," Kassidy suddenly says. I can tell she's lying by the uncomfortable look on her face. Damn Aimee for showing up when she did.

I rise from my seat as Kassidy stands. She turns to leave when Aimee mouths off, "What bargain store did your assistant buy her suit from? It looks like something my maid would wear to clean my parents' house."

"Excuse me," Kassidy whirls on her heels and backtracks to face a blue-eyed, red-faced Aimee.

"Aimee was just leaving." I give my ex-fuck-buddy a pointed glance. "I will be right back Kassidy." I turn and grab Aimee by the arm and drag her away from my assistant and out into the lobby.

"Let me go. You're squeezing my arm too tight!"

I immediately release her. "What gives you the right to interrupt my lunch acting superior to my assistant and treating her in such a condescending manner?"

"I'm sorry," she sidles up to me and tries to wrap her arms around my neck.

"Back off Aimee. The arrangement between the

two of us is over. Don't call, don't come by my home or office, or you will be thrown out by security."

"Nikolai! I said I was sorry," she whines. Why are you treating me like this over some black—"

"Don't even go there. Shut the fuck up while you're ahead," I growl softly against her ear. "Do I make myself clear?"

"Yes," she nods and I stand to my full height.

"Good," I mutter and walk off and back to my table, but my assistant is nowhere in sight.

"Miss Davis said to tell you she went back to the office," the waiter tells me.

"Thanks, I'm ready to settle the bill," I tell him.

"The bill has been taken care of by Miss Davis."

Shit... Kassidy must have left out at the side exit. I pull out my slim wallet and remove a fifty dollar bill. "Thanks for your help," I tip the waiter.

"You're welcome and thank you sir! Would you like me to box up your meals?"

"No, that won't be necessary," I reply as I turn and stroll out the restaurant.

I unclip my cell phone and shoot Kassidy a quick text.

Never walk out on me again. Got that Miss Davis?

I'm half way back to the office before I receive a reply.

Yes sir Mr. Pierce. I got it loud and clear.

I grin at my assistant's quick reply. It appears that I'm going to have to work for what I want. Good —game on.

CHAPTER SEVEN

Kassidy

LATER THAT EVENING

The Chinese restaurant is filled to capacity. I glance around the room hoping we can find a seat. I notice an older couple is just finishing up their meals.

"Give me three minutes and I will get you two seated," says the waitress.

Anita and I make small talk while we wait. Before long, we are seated and our plates are filled from the all you can eat Chinese buffet.

"Thank you Anita for treating me to a celebratory dinner."

"You're welcome. I need for you to know that I support your choices. So, how did things go today?"

I take a drink from my wine glass and pull myself away from my most inner thoughts to focus on my friend.

"It was good," I sigh, squeezing my thighs together thinking about my two fine young bosses. My thirty plus year old ass should feel ashamed for even thinking about my employers in that way, but all I feel is fierce lust.

"Hmm, what are you not telling me heffa?" Nita asks.

"Whatever do you mean?"

"Ugh! Does it look like I fell off a turnip truck? Something juicy happened on your first week at work and you're keeping it to yourself. That's no fair, we tell each other everything. I'm the sister by another mother you never had, remember?"

I chuckle, taking another sip from my glass of fruity wine. "Okay, I'll tell you but stop acting like you are twelve. Sheesh!"

My friend pours herself another glass of wine and settles back against the chair.

"First tell me is N&D Inc. as nice inside as the Fortune 100 magazine depicts?"

"Oh my God, yes! The building and the offices are massive, with high towering ceilings at least fifty feet high. Each floor has its own receptionist and secretary. The floor I work on has its own private balcony that extends from my bosses offices.

"Hmm, Kass did you just say bosses, as in two of them?"

"Yep. N&D has two CEOs. Nikolai and Dirk built their company from the ground up and you won't believe how young they are!" I finish off the last of my wine as heat intensifies between my thighs at the mere thought of them.

"Damn. You are a lucky woman. Honey, are your new bosses sexy and how young are they?" My friend scoots to the edge of her seat sending me a curious look.

"Trust me, they are too young for you to be looking at me in that way."

Nita lets loose a boisterous laugh. "There is nothing wrong with thinking younger men are sexy, as long as they are legal. Since they both are owners of successful businesses and both finished Yale at the top of their class, I am assuming both are grown ass men."

"They are in their late twenties."

"Well, you're good."

"Huh—"

"Your two bosses are fine. You haven't been laid in forever. I'm sure your coochie has cobwebs by now. Make it happen with one or both of them Kass. Then tell me every delicious detail."

I place my empty wine glass on the table in front of me. I stand to my feet and start looking under my chair. I'm too tipsy to care about the curious glances thrown my way.

"Um, Kassidy, what are you doing?"

"Ha! I am trying to see where you lost your brains so that I can give them back to you."

"Woman sit your ass down," Nita smirks. "Very funny though, but I'm serious. I read that those two have a reputation for being on the wild side."

"That doesn't mean that they will be wild with me. I am black and they are both--"

"Stop right there lady. I know what you are going to say. You are a smart, independent, beautiful woman and that's all any man will see, no matter the color or the age."

"Seriously, you don't know them and I'm not their type. I saw Nikolai's type earlier today when he took me to lunch. She was pale as he was, and petite."

"Wait, you had lunch with your boss?"

"Well sort of--"

"What do you mean sort of?" Anita's eyes narrows on me.

"I didn't finish my lunch because my boss had to see to his girlfriend or whatever she was, so I paid for our meals and left."

"No you didn't!"

"Yes, I did. I think my bosses will be all business. I must keep it professional if I want to keep this job. You already know how much I wanted this job. I can't, and won't, mess it up with my lustful fantasies."

"See! I knew it. You are fucking hot for your new bosses."

I couldn't fool Anita if I tried. She knows me too well. Anita has known me long enough to know when something is bothering me, or even when I'm trying to hide something from her. It's the same for me when it comes to her. This reinforces our bond of friendship.

"They are hot," I finally admit it out loud. "They're both tall, broad and muscular. Plus they smell delicious."

"I'm so jealous right now. I want to be you," laughs Anita. "You, me, Octavia, and Leelayna need to get together and celebrate."

"Yeah, that would be great, but right now no more talk about my job. Tell me everything about your day," I say, trying to change the subject. While I sit and half listen to Anita chatter, I have the audacity to silently wonder what my bosses bulging muscles looks like beneath their expensive suits.

I surmise basically, my two new employers are sex on a stick and I want to taste them both. *Lord have mercy!* I need another drink. I must quit thinking like this or it will be the end of my time at

N&D Incorporated. I exhale and give myself a mental shake.

I can hear my brain telling me that even though I find my bosses sexy as hell. That doesn't mean I have to make a damn fool of myself by acting like a young teen around them. I'm a new employee and I'm sure some other person will be ready to snatch this position up at a moment's notice if I fail. I will smile, do my job, keep my fucking hormones under wraps, and be the dutiful employee that I am.

CHAPTER EIGHT

Kassidy

The buzzing of my digital clock awakes me. "Today is the start of my second week at N&D, and I declare it will be great," I say aloud as I rise in bed and look towards the window. The sun is seeping through a slit in the curtain. I wish I could sleep in as I press the snooze button on the clock and plop back on my fluffy pillows. *No can do!* I reason with myself and then roll over to switch off the alarm clock and push the bedcovers off my body. I sit up in bed once again and stretch, stifling a yawn with my hand cupped over my mouth. Sliding out of bed I make my way to the bathroom to take care of my business and then take a quick shower.

Noticing the time, I quickly grab a towel to dry

myself, lotion my body and slip into the outfit I had chosen the night before. The time is now almost seven thirty, and I know I need to hurry and hope my car doesn't give me any trouble. I've only just got the job at N&D Inc.; I don't need to be late. I need to prove myself a valuable employee if I don't want my bosses to regret hiring me.

Thank God! My car starts and I'm heading to work with time to spare. Breathing a sigh of relief, I settle in at my desk and start my day. I make sure to check the emails first and send out the required responses. Next, I glance at the contract on my desk that needs to be signed by Nikolai. There is a note to fax it to him. I feel a little disappointed that I won't have to walk it to his office and see him face to face. However, I could use a cup of coffee. I decide to go to the break area before faxing over the contract for Nikolai's signature. God knows I need to be full of clarity to get through my day.

The break area is relatively empty except for two other women standing around talking. "Good morning," I murmur heading over to the coffee machine.

"Good morning," the two women reply in unison.

"I'm Bailey, and this is Vanna," says the brunette. "You must be the new assistant for Nikolai and Dirk?"

"I'm Kassidy, and yes, I am," I reply grabbing a plastic cup and pouring a cup of coffee. I add a couple of packs of sugar and a dollop of cream before stirring it and taking a tentative sip of the hot brew.

"You better be on your A game. Nikolai and Dirk are hard men to work for— or so I heard," giggles Vanna.

"Hard or not, I would take my chances with either or both of them," Bailey adds giving me the once over.

I bristle inwardly from her scrutiny. I need to go shopping for some new clothes but my finances don't allow that kind of luxury yet. First, I have to work on getting my car in tip-top shape and then maybe I can splurge a little on getting a new wardrobe.

"Did you hear about the rumor?" Vanna turns towards Bailey with a sly smile on her face.

"What rumor?" Bailey answers. I know I should get back to work, but these two gossiping women pique my interest.

"I hear the only reason that Nola quit working for Nikolai and Dirk is that her husband got jealous."

Bailey's blue eyes sparkle with interest at this bit of information.

"I figured as much. Almost all of the women here want to sleep with them. Married or unmarried," Bailey goes on to say. "Both men are gorgeous and rich, who wouldn't want to wake up in their beds every morning?"

"Hell yeah, I know I would. It would be easy to

accommodate both of them in a heartbeat," Vanna adds. As if remembering that I was in the break area, the two women look at me as if I don't belong.

I wonder if it's true. *Did Mr. Pierce and Mr. Hawkings attempt to break up their assistant's marriage? What kind of men would try to do something like that?*

"Well Kassidy, are you married?" Bailey asks.

"No, I'm—"

"Married or not, you won't have anything to worry about. You are far from their type," this comes from the woman named Vanna.

"Listen, I came here to work. I don't give a damn about being their type or not," I lied. "My only focus is to work, get a paycheck and go home. I agree with you; I'm sure you two are more the bosses speed." I walk over to the sink and pour out the rest of my coffee before walking out of the break room and quickly back to my office.

Get back to work Kassidy, I tell myself. *You don't have the time to be entertaining office gossip.*

About fifteen minutes after I'm back in my office, I look up through the transparent wall of my office and see the elevator open. A second later, Nikolai walks off and our eyes lock in a stare. He nods his head slightly and greets me with a charming grin. I bow my head back and return a friendly smile.

CHAPTER NINE

Nikolai

"**K**assidy Davis."

The thick, sexy, baritone voice of Nikolai booms out my name, and a tremble goes through my entire system. I force myself to glance up, toward the office door.

I allow my eyes to look directly into his, and my heart beats rapidly against my breastbone. Nikolai's eyes pierce into me, even from where he's standing. His suit fits the vast expanse of his broad shoulders impeccably well. He is wearing a dark gray vest underneath a custom made white shirt that can be seen from beneath the jacket. His jawline is chiseled and square cut, with a day's old shadow covering his jawline.

I breathe intensely as I stand to my feet. "Do you need to see me sir?"

"Come to my office, now," he states before turning and walking back into his office, leaving the door ajar for me to follow.

I hope that I haven't done anything wrong.

I grab my notepad and pen then head to Nikolai's office. I'm nervous as hell considering the way his voice sounded. I enter my boss's office and scan his face to get a read on his mood.

"Why are you just standing there? Come in and have a seat."

I give a tentative smile and walk over to have a seat in front of his desk.

"I haven't had a chance to talk to you about the lunch you aborted the other week. Aimee was an old acquaintance of mine. She means nothing to me. Don't ever walk out on me again Kassidy. Do I make myself clear?"

I fidget in my seat and avoid eye contact. Nikolai's voice is firm and brooks no argument, but his eyes are fire and ice burning me alive.

"Yes sir," I nod in agreement.

"Kassidy, look at me." My gaze instantly drifts back to his face.

"Okay, let's try this again. Meet me out front at

noon; a car will be waiting to take us to a restaurant for lunch."

"Yes, sir. Is that all?"

"Call me Nikolai, remember? Also, that will be all for now."

"All right Nikolai. I'll meet you out front at noon."

I stood, rushed out of his office, and didn't breathe until I made it back to my desk.

When Nikolai and I arrived for lunch at a trendy restaurant in downtown at the Eastside business district, I had no idea that French food smelled so good. Nikolai and I ordered the French Fusion Braised Chicken dinner. It is some of the best chicken I'd ever eaten. I have to admit that I am enjoying myself.

I made sure I stuck to one glass of wine because I didn't want to get tipsy.

"So, this time around isn't so bad is it?"

"No, I'm sorry that I walked out on you before. That wasn't very professional, and you have every right to fire me," I say looking down to avoid Nikolai's silvery glance.

"Why would I fire you when I'm trying to know you better? Plus, you've proven to be a great employee so far."

A surprised breath escapes my lips before I mutter a soft, "Thank you." I take another sip from my wine glass before speaking again. "Know me how?" I query.

"How does a man usually want to know a woman Kassidy?" Suddenly, a charming grin lights up his handsome face. "Eat up! We have plenty of time to know one another fully."

"Do you want dessert?" he asks after a while, glancing at the desserts on display.

"I better not—"

"Nonsense," he says signaling for the dessert server. "What tickles your fancy?" he asks.

"I'll take a red velvet cupcake."

"What will you have sir?" the server asks.

"Nothing for me," Nikolai replies as I bite into my cupcake.

"Wow, these are delicious. You should have gotten one."

"I would rather have a bite of yours," Nikolai retorts with a salacious grin.

I lean over and offer him a bite of the sweet treat from the unbitten side, but he takes my wrist in his hand and twists it to the side I had already taken a bite from. Nikolai licked his lips and it made my pussy throb.

"You're right, that is delicious. There is only one thing I know that tastes better," Nikolai says with a naughty gleam in his eyes.

I gulp and pray I can get through the rest of the lunch while retaining my professionalism.

Dirk

I scowl at Nikolai before joining him in watching as Kassidy gathers her things and leaves for the day. I close my eyes and imagine me tasting her succulent pussy with the scent of her arousal cloaked around me. Damn, the thought of us together had me rock hard.

"That's why you've been grouchy as a bear. You want her same as I do," Nikolai chuckles as we both watch Kassidy walk towards the elevator. Her curvaceous ass sways, and I grow harder.

"Did you make a move on her at lunch today?" I ask Nikolai.

"Of course, I did. I wanted to stretch Kassidy across the table, fuck her, and claim her as mine. Those dark brown eyes, plump lips, and the hint of her voluptuous breasts beneath the prim blouse she wore nearly had me taking her there on the spot. Damn, who saw us."

Shit. I know precisely the way Nikolai feels. I wanted Kassidy the first moment she walked into my office. Her big boobs and well-rounded ass made my cock hard as granite. My blood pounds through my veins as the truth spill from my lips.

"I want her," I growled softly.

Nikolai grinned, our eyes met once Kassidy stepped in the elevator, and the doors closed behind her. "I want her too. We can both have her if we play our cards right. Stop being so mean to her, or you might scare her away," Nikolai warned.

"Fuck. I know it. Wanting her in this way frustrates the hell out of me. I have never felt this way about another woman before," I say, raking a hand through my hair.

"That's because she's our mate, bro," Nikolai replies in a matter of fact tone.

"So, do you think Kassidy is the one?"

"I don't just think it. I know it. And Dirk, if you were honest with yourself, you already know it too."

Nikolai knows me too well just as I know him. "You are damn right, I know it."

Nikolai chuckled and slapped me on the back. Let's get out of here and get a drink. We can grab a steak too. All of a sudden, I feel ravenous."

"Sounds like a plan," I reply, walking over to grab my suit jacket and put it on.

Before long, Nikolai and I left the building and headed over to Smokestack Lounge Bar and Grill.

We entered the building and were seated almost immediately. We were sitting at our usual table, and soon had rare steaks, baked potatoes, mixed steamed vegetables, and a whiskey before each of us.

"What's bothering you?" Nikolai asks.

"How do you think Kassidy will feel when she finds out who we are?" I ask Nikolai.

Nikolai remains quiet for a moment. "I think Kassidy will be open-minded and accept us for who we are."

"I hope you're right. Being the triad for the Edgewood Growlers takes a special kind of woman."

"Trust me, our hunting ends with Kassidy Davis," Nikolai says, cutting into his steak. The juices from the steak ran red.

I dug into my own, taking a bite.

The Omega in me growled inwardly at the thought of Kassidy becoming ours. Nikolai, the Alpha, is sure of Kassidy, and now after much thought, I am too.

Nikolai isn't only my best friend; he's like a brother to me. There is nothing we don't share. We have shared women in the past, but this time the woman will be different. She will be our mate. Kassidy will be the one connection as Omega and Alpha, bringing us closer together than we have ever been before.

We were never lucky enough to find a mate in the Edgewood Pack. None of the women ever came close to Kassidy or the need she arises within us. The kind of woman we want needs to be accessible to a committed relationship with the two of us, making us a nexus of three. Kassidy would be just as crucial as Nikolai's Alpha and just as expressive as me once our connection is united.

"Are you ready to make Kassidy ours?" Nikolai asks.

"You're damn straight, I am. Let's do this!" I reply and we clink our whiskey tumblers together to seal the deal of making Kassidy Davis delightfully ours.

CHAPTER TEN

Kassidy

A FEW DAYS LATER

"Thanks girl, for meeting me this evening," I say to Anita as we sit at a table at the Zin Zam Bar and Lounge.

"No problem, honey. I can use a drink or three after the day I had."

"That bad, huh?" I ask.

"Yeah," Anita replies just as the waitress arrives to take our orders.

"What can I get for you ladies?" the waitress asks.

"I would like a quarter pound sirloin burger with the sweet potato fries," I waste no time in placing my order. I already knew what I wanted when I arrived.

"I will have the same," pipes in Anita.

"What to drink?" the waitress asks.

"I will have a Pink Lady of Montenegro," I say of the cocktail that contains a mixture of rum, grilled strawberry, lime, and Amaro. "Order anything you want Anita. Tonight is my treat.

"I'll have the cranberry and vodka," Anita adds. "Thanks, my friend!" She gives me a big smile that I readily return.

"Great! I'll return with your meals and drinks soon," the waitress replies before strolling off to fulfill our orders.

"So, what's going on with your job? Are you acclimating well?"

I let out a long breath. "Nita, I don't know if I'm going or coming at times. Whenever I'm around Nikolai or Dirk, it feels as if I'm stepping into a fiery furnace."

"That's because you have the hots for your two billionaire Alpha bosses. The sooner you admit it, the better off you will be, honey."

"That's just it, I do feel a strong chemistry with both of them. Even though Dirk acts like an ass most times, I still feel strongly attracted to him. But, I have no room in my life for complications."

"Kass, I understand. It's best to not mix business with pleasure. Those rules, spoken or unspoken, are in place for a reason. But you know me, I don't give a shit about the rules. Life is too short. Let loose, and—"

"Here are your orders," the waitress places our meals and drinks on the table cutting off Anita's words.

"Thank you," we say in unison.

"Enjoy your meal and if you need anything else just let me know."

We nod and wait until the waitress leaves before resuming our conversation.

"Now, what was I saying?" Anita bites into her burger while I stuff a fry in my mouth.

"You were saying something about letting loose."

"Oh yeah! Kass, you need to not think so hard. I would give an arm for two hot men to set their sights on me."

"I'm not one hundred percent sure that they have set their sights on me. Do you remember me telling you about that Terrance guy that I thought was interested in me when I was in college?"

"Yeah, I remember," Anita grins and arches a brow inquiringly.

"Well, I thought he liked me— I mean a lot. We even went out on a couple of dates. I was devastated when he said he loved being my friend and could I set him up with my roommate, Evect."

"Terrance was a jerk to string you along just to get close to your roommate. Why didn't he just talk to her himself instead of getting you in the middle?" Anita gives me a disgruntled look. "He was a lowlife bastard if you ask me."

"I agree. Anyway, Evect had a boyfriend that went to a different University that she was devoted to since she was sixteen years old. Terrance wanted me to sway her into giving him a chance even though she was otherwise committed."

"God damn fucking piece of shit!" Anita says angrily.

"My thoughts exactly. Then came my most recent breakup with Stanley. I thought he really loved me. Damn, Anita, I'm thirty-two years old, and I'm still reading men wrong. Look how he dumped me for someone younger and—"

"Don't you even say it, Kass. Stanley is another piece of shit that you need to forget. Just think of him as another bump in the road and move the hell on."

"You're right about that. Anyhow, the more that I think about it, Stanley and I weren't even compatible. I think I even liked him more than I loved him."

A sly grin forms on Anita's face. "Have fun with your two bosses. Subtly flirt and see who takes the bait. What's living without taking chances?"

I let out a chuckle; I've always liked Anita's way of thinking, but I'm not a flirter like she is. It comes naturally to her. I've taken going into relationships seriously. I want to be married one day soon. Maybe have a couple of kids. But that's not going to happen until the right man comes along that wants the same things as I do. I have to get over this crush, or whatever it is I feel for my bosses. Dirk and Nikolai are ruthless businessmen. They may be younger than me, but they are dynamic in the business world and are respected by the masses.

"Do you want another drink?" I ask Anita.

"Sure," she replies, and I signal to the waiter to place a refill on our drinks.

"Stop stressing girl," she tells me.

"I am not stressing," I answer without looking at her.

"Liar! I know stressing. You've gone all quiet; I can hear the thoughts mulling around in that head of yours." Anita gives me a big smile and taps the side of her head; I laugh.

Soon the waitress comes back and places fresh drinks on the table. I will be sure to leave her a good tip.

"Okay, maybe I am stressing a little, but I will be alright. I just need to chill and keep things in perspective."

"And that is," Anita prompts me to finish my sentence.

"I just need to go to work, do my job, get paid and go home. Simple as that."

"Get real, Kass! You know as well as I do that life is not simple. It's made of various complexities to rain on our parade."

I glance at Anita from the corner of my eye. I take a long sip from my drink before speaking, "But I crave simplicity in my life."

Anita shrugs her thin shoulders. "Well my friend, we don't always get what we wish for," she replies smoothly.

"I know that only too well." I sigh and finish my meal.

"Kass, you know I want the best for you, right?"

"Girl I already know that. I want the best for you too," I smile.

Anita and I finish our meals and part ways in the parking lot with the promise of being in touch soon.

As I drive home, I think about how even after three weeks into my new job, I still feel disheartened and confused. Regardless of the talk I had with Anita, I've come to the decision that this is a problem I must work through in one way or another myself. Being practical is the way to go.

CHAPTER ELEVEN

Kassidy

I'm so glad to be home, although, having dinner with my friend was mostly pleasant. I silently think about the night as I turn on the shower and adjust the temperature. The warm water invigorates me immediately as the shower head that hangs above sprays water onto my body, helping my muscles relax. I hope to have someone to come home to— to share my life with. I've never been a promiscuous person. I've only been with two men sexually. One during my college years and sadly to say Stanley had been my last. Wetness brims in my eyes and spills down my cheeks. I pinch my lips together trying to stop the onslaught of emotions running through me. It must be the drinks I had earlier tonight that are making these vulnerabilities rise within me.

I sniff as I try not to cry and reach for the body gel to pour onto a washcloth.

I run the soap over my entire body; the action soothing to my skin. I run the washcloth over my breasts and suck in my breath when my nipple pebbles. I close my eyes, and my two bosses emerge in my thoughts. The soap caressing my flesh like gentle kisses, and my pussy throbs with need. It's been so long since a man made love to me. An overwhelming demand infuses me with desire. Me touching myself like I always do isn't enough anymore. I crave to be loved by two men.

I feel ashamed to admit that fact, even to myself. More tears escaped my eyes from the frustration of it all. I hurry and finish my shower, dry off, and moisturize my skin before sliding into bed.

The images of my dream immediately run through my head. I imagine both Dirk and Nikolai in my bed having their way with me. I allow my hands to roam down my stomach before moving down to my splayed thighs. One finger touches and circles my slick clitoris while another finger delves deep inside my wet core, wishing it was a cock. I bite my lip to hold back a moan and writhe my hips up, down and around on the bed.

My breathing becomes quick, and my moans

emerge in gasps. I rub my nub faster and faster. I allow one hand to squeeze my breast and pinch my nipple. My hips continue to move up and down. My chest aches from me craving the touch of Nikolai and Dirk. I want and need more than my damn fingers.

I reach over in my bedside drawer and grab my vibrating dildo. The head of the dildo is bulbous, smooth, and round at the end. A perfect replacement since I don't have the real thing.

I throw my legs in the air and shove the phallus inside my throbbing core. A moan escapes my lips as I feel my insides cling to the dildo and pulse around it. I slide the dildo in and out of my wetness, moving my hips to a rhythm.

"Oh my God, Nikolai! Fuck me, Dirk!" I cry out, feeling the intensity of an orgasm growing inside my wet heat.

My hips keep pumping as I push the dildo inside me repeatedly. Pleasure electrocutes my body from head to toe as I cum with a loud scream.

Electrical shocks hold me suspended with intense desire for a minute before it releases me from its grasp. I pant trying to get my breathing under control. I pull the dildo out before laying it on the bedside table. *I'll clean it in the morning*— I thought before rolling over and falling into a satisfied sleep.

CHAPTER TWELVE

Kassidy

M*y friends Octavia Smith, Anita Holley, and Leelayna Hinton, sit at a table in the Inferno Lounge. As usual, Anita is the life of the bunch. We have three shots of tequila each sitting in front of us. The club is dim with flashing lights of blue and red, but the atmosphere completely shields me from the reality of having to think of getting dumped by a loser like Stanley.*

"Let's drink to Kassidy's new found freedom. I always knew that Stanley was a rotten, low-down womanizer bastard anyway. Trust me on this Kassidy, he didn't deserve a good faithful woman like you."

"I agree," our friend Anita joins in. "Stanley is a

pompous ass with a stick up his butt. You can do better sweetheart," she gives me a look of sympathy.

"I'll drink to that," I plaster on a smile and pick up a shot glass. I bring the glass to my lips and throw back its contents in one gulp.

"Shit! That's some good stuff," Octavia says. She's the flirtiest of my three friends. She never dates just one man because she says when one acts a fool there is always another one on hand. Hell, maybe she's right. Some men can be such dirty dogs. Stanley just happens to be leading the pack.

"I feel for you, Kass," Octavia chimes in. "You remember that I went through a bad breakup with Donnie last year. He was sleeping around with multiple women. I was so stressed... That's when I lost our baby," Octavia says.

"Humph, Donnie was, and still is, a complete ass. He was an even bigger cheater than Stanley," Anita responds. "I'm sorry you had a miscarriage, Octavia, but maybe it was for the best. You would have had to be tied to Donnie for at least the next eighteen years. Now you're free of his lies and cheating ways."

"Yes, I agree," Octavia coincides. Anita bobs her head to the music and takes a sip of her drink. "You two need new men in your lives ASAP." She adjusts her low cut clingy dress over her boobs.

I remain silent, but I reach over and give Anita's

hand a comforting squeeze. I don't let on, but I have no plans to date anytime soon.

Anita's eyes meet mine and she gives me a slight smile. I can tell the lingering effect of her pain still affects her deeply. I wonder when my own heart will stop hurting. It's been three weeks since my ex fiancé trampled all over my heart.

"Hey, I have an idea," Octavia claims, snagging my attention.

"What is your brilliant idea?" I tease her.

"Let's dance!" she says and hops up from the table.

"Great idea!" Leelayna chimes in. My friends seem to be on one accord except me. I look out at the crowded dance floor and watch the gyrating bodies move to the constant beat of the music. The couples are flowing in nimble arcs, bodies in continuous rhythmic motion, to the loud beat of the music.

"You all go ahead. I'll join you later. I'm going to the bar to get another drink," I tell them.

"Okay, but hurry," Anita adds before they take off towards the dance floor. I stand and head towards the bar.

I had just made it to the bar and was trying to get the busy bartender's attention when I hear a baritone voice beside me speak. My head whips around and I crane my neck to look up into the man's face.

"Hello beautiful," a voice that remind me of Dirk's

says over the chatter and loud music going on around us. He leans over closer to me to be heard and the aroma of his smell makes me want to swoon. I grab the edge of the bar to help me remain on my feet.

I turn and look up at one of my gorgeous bosses. My mind silently screams, I must be dreaming! I gulp in awe. Is Dirk Hawkings really here looking at me as if he could gobble me up?

My attention focuses on his eyes, then trails down to his broad shoulders. A deep growling sound eases from his mouth. My eyes widen and I peer up into his gorgeous face. Shivers travel all over my body. Suddenly, I feel a bump from my other side. I jerk my head around and Nikolai is standing beside me.

"Ahem," I try to swallow the sudden lump in my throat. I'm wedged between two gorgeous giants at the bar. Things like this never ever happens to me. I can feel a trickle of sweat ease between the valley of my breast area.

"Hello beautiful, what are you doing here? I'm happy to see you here though," Nikolai says giving me an expectant look.

"Umm—" I pause for a moment because I can't seem to gather my thoughts. I nibble on my bottom lip, and this time I hear a growl escape Nikolai's lips. "I'm here with some friends," I sputter out fast. I inhale and a

spicy, exotic scent unlike any I've smelled before assaults my nostrils from Nikolai.

"Cool. I hope you can ditch them for a while and spend some time with Dirk and me. Now what about letting me and Dirk buy you a couple of drinks?" His succulent lips curves into a sexy smile.

"Oh okay," my voice squeaks out on a high note. My cheeks flush, but I'm glad my dark brown color and the dim lightening surrounding us hides the flush that spreads across my cheeks.

"What will you have, lovely lady?" Nikolai asks.

"I was drinking tequila, so I'll stick with that," I glance over my shoulder, and I am met with the stare of all my friends. Anita is giving me a thumbs up, and the others are smiling and giving me the look of encouragement.

Nikolai gets the bartender's attention and orders tequila shots for the three of us. My focus is on my crazy friends and their antics.

"Here you go sweetheart," Dirk's deep voice causes me to focus on him once again. I turn around just as the bartender sets a shot of tequila on the bar area.

"Thanks for the drink bosses, but I need to get back to my friends. I was supposed to place our drink orders."

"No problem. What are your friends having?" asks Nikolai.

"*The same as me. Tequila shots,*" *I reply.*

"*Hey bartender, give our girl Kassidy and her friends anything they ask for. Put it on my tab,*" *he directs.*

"*No, you don't have—*"

"*Hey, come and dance with me,*" *Dirk directs. He doesn't wait for me to answer. Dirk just takes my hand in his and pulls me out towards the dance floor. I become warm all over when he takes me into his arms, moving seductively. My eyes shut as his heady aroma fills my nostrils, and we sway to the seductive music piping from the surround sound speakers in the ceiling.*

My eyes pop open when I fill another warm body pressing up against my backside.

"*Wait, wha—*" *I start to say, but Nikolai bends down near my ear with his mouth. His breath smells like mint mixed with tequila.*

"*Don't be afraid. Dirk and I got you,*" *he tells me pressing up closer against me. I suddenly feel faint being sandwiched between all this testosterone. One slow song spins into the next. The dance floor is already crammed with couples. The music is sensually soft, and I'm melting like hot caramel between these two tall, muscular bodies.*

This is crazy! How can this be happening with my two employers?

I try to crane my neck to look up into Dirk's face, but my eyes meet only the open neckline of his chest. Oh God! I almost blurt out when I feel twin erections pressing into my flesh. One hard as steel shaft is pushed into my belly and the other is lodged at the split of my ass. The tension in my body temperature is rising along with my arousal. I can't believe I'm dancing with two men like this. This has never ever happened to me in all of my thirty-two years on this earth. I must be in paradise.

Nikolai leans down, pressing his body even tighter against my back.

"Babe," Nikolai murmurs against my ear, "you need to relax and go with the flow."

I gasp. My breathing becomes ragged.

"Yeah, sweetheart. Relax and enjoy. There's so much that Nikolai and I want to do to you," Dirk leans in near my other ear and speaks. Then his tongue plunges inside and begins to swirl. My mouth opens, and soft moans slip past my lips. My thong instantly becomes saturated with my juices. Nikolai takes that moment to slide a hand down my back to the curve of my ass and squeeze.

"Fuck!" Nikolai growls like a feral animal. "You have a lot of ass, and I love every inch of it."

"Oh," my moan is prolonged into a satisfying sigh.

"Do you feel what you do to us, Kassidy? Do you know how long we've been searching for the woman that we can share?" Dirk brushes his lips against my cheek. I shiver and become lost in a whirlwind of wanting.

"Babe, I'm so fucking hard right now. You are fucking beautiful," he adds. "I can even smell your arousal," Dirk sniffs the air.

"She smells like peaches and cream, doesn't she?" Nikolai growls.

"Shit! We need to get the fuck out of here before we have our way with her on the dance floor." Nikolai and Dirk talk back and forth over my head. I feel as if I'm caught up in an alternate universe.

I open my mouth to speak and try to gather enough strength to push against Dirk's chest, but I'm too over-whelmed with lust. I try to gain my composure.

"I must have a taste." I'm suddenly turned around, and now I'm facing Nikolai. His mouth slams down on mine, I can't help but release another gasp. Nikolai takes this opportunity to plunge his minty tongue into my mouth. Our mouths mesh together and instant warmth spreads through my veins. Nikolai grunts in the back of his throat. The growly grunt he makes sounds so damn sexy. Dirk is gripping my waistline in a posses-sive grip.

"Damn it. I ache to be deep inside you, Kass. I want

to fuck your pussy until you cream all over my cock. Then I want to taste your sweetness," Dirk grunts out near my ear. My head is spinning, my body is getting ready to detonate. Nikolai fucks my mouth continuously with his tongue. I can feel Dirk's shaft pulsing with a thump— thump against my butt.

"Hmm, I can't wait for Dirk and me to have our way with you once we get you home," Nikolai grumbles. Just when I didn't think I could get any wetter; I have to squeeze my thighs together to keep moisture from escaping my underwear.

"I think we can use a little more privacy," Dirk suggests. The music switches to an up tempo beat.

"You're reading my mind," Nikolai agrees. I feel adrift when their bodies ease away from me. Then instantly I become settled again when Nikolai places his hand at the small of my back and Dirk grasps my right hand. They direct me to a dim vacant room that's up a flight of stairs in the Lounge.

"Wait, where are we going?"

"Don't worry, Nikolai and I are silent partners in the Inferno. We just want to be alone with you for a bit without the crowd. Don't be afraid, I promise we won't hurt you."

"Do you trust us?" Dirk cut in. I'm pressed between the two of them before I can formulate a reply.

"I— I..."

"You are sweet torture; do you know that?" Nikolai asks, bending to nuzzle my neck.

I'm melting like sweet buttercream, but unbeknownst to them, they are sweet torture to me as well. I have to shake myself out of this drunken sexual haze that's tempting me to be all kinds of wrong. The temptation is a mother fucker, I think to myself.

"Um, Nikolai and Dirk, you're both too gorgeous, and sexy for your own good," I say. *They smell divine, I add silently.* *"But you're both my employers. I'm your employee. We can't be doing this. I've never been a promiscuous woman in my life."*

"We know you, Kass. Dirk and I knew the instant you walked into N&D that you belonged to us," Nikolai says.

"Wha—"

"Shhh, listen to us for a minute and please keep an open mind sweetheart. We are going to tell you something about the two of us, but we need you to promise that you won't be afraid of us. I promise you; we will never do anything to hurt you. We will spend our life loving you," Dirk says.

"I think I'm dreaming," I reply as I look between the two giant men standing before me. *"These types of things don't happen to me."*

"I understand what we are about to say to you may be overwhelming," Dirk takes me by the hand and leads

me over to sit on a plush looking sofa situated in the center of the room. He sits down on my right side and Nikolai comes to stand in front of me before he begins to pace. He reminds me of a wild, feral beast about to pounce. I shiver at the thought.

I breathe harshly, looking between the two before nervously nibbling on my bottom lip. A deep scratching noise unlike any I'd heard before leaves Nikolai's throat. Alarmed by the lusty, throaty noise, I look up at him. The sounds deepen coming from his throat. Its savage, primal sound has me pressing my back into Dirk. He is seated next to me as if he's my protection. Dirk's muscular arms envelop me, but I can't take my eyes off Nikolai.

Nikolai's eyes never leave mine. "I think I better leave," I stutter as I attempt to rise from the sofa, but Dirk's arms tighten around my waist. Suddenly, a strange growling noise sounds directly behind me. The feral noise, which comes from Dirk, makes me wetter. Whipping my head around, I notice the same desirous look from Dirk's eyes that's in Nikolai's.

"Fuck, Kassidy. I can smell your pussy's arousal for us. Don't be afraid," Dirk growls out.

I nibble on my bottom lip so hard that it bleeds. "I really need to go. My friends are worried about me. They will come looking for me, you know," I give them both a warning, but it didn't seem to faze either one of them.

"Let me take care of that for you, sweetness," Nikolai says as he sat down on the other side of me. Nikolai closes the space between us as he comes closer with his eyes on my mouth. Nikolai proceeds to lick my bottom lip before forcing his tongue into my mouth. "Delicious," he mutters, and I moan aloud.

"Give me a taste of your lips." Dirk yanks me away from Nikolai and turns me in his direction. Before I can say anything, his lips slams down on mine, capturing me in a pussy wetting kiss.

My arms wrap around Dirk's neck on their own volition. Nikolai presses against my back and begins nibbling and sucking my earlobe into his warm mouth. I don't know how much more of their seduction that I'll be able to take. My core pulses with intensity. I squeeze my thighs together trying to assuage the throb.

"Sweet heaven," I sigh.

"Kassidy my love, tell us what you want." Dirk places kisses all over my face, and then hones in on my lips again. He pulls me down as he lies back onto the armrest of the sofa. Nikolai seems to be in sync with Dirk's positioning me because he backs away until Dirk has me settled between his thighs. The bold imprint of his cock has me gasping. My wet sex is in direct contact with Dirk's humongous hardon. Dirk's mouth catches each of my lusty sighs since he never released my lips.

Nikolai settles at my backside again. I can tell

Nikolai is holding his weight off me with a forearm. Suddenly, Nikolai's teeth sink into my shoulder through the material of my thin clingy dress.

"Ah," I cry out. I no longer care if making out with two men makes me sluttish. I want both Dirk and Nikolai more than I've ever wanted any other men. More than I've ever wanted Stanley. Stanley Jones paled in my memory the more I get caught up in these two gorgeous men's seduction.

"Do you want us to make love to you, Kassidy?" Nikolai's deep voice growls out.

Dirk takes that moment to grab my covered breast. His teeth sink down on my hard nipple as he licks, sucks and bites through the material of my dress and lace bra.

"Oh my God, yes!" I shout as I start to become delirious.

Nikolai rocks his erection into the crack of my rounded ass. He's hard as granite, and I can feel him pulsing, even through his slacks. A fiery lust sizzles through every nerve of my body. I crave to be filled fully inside my heated core.

"We won't take you here. We want you spread out on our bed where we can take our time feasting over every inch of your body. Do you agree, Nikolai?"

"My thoughts exactly, my friend," Nikolai agrees.

Nikolai licks my neckline before sucking my tender flesh into his mouth. At the same time, Dirk's teeth sink into the opposite part of my neck. I let loose a whaling whine. My hips grind into Dirk's shaft while my ass bumps into Nikolai's erection with each upward motion.

"That's it, sweetheart, cum for us," Dirk urges. I feel a hand lift my dress; it slides further up my thigh and fingers hook beneath my soaking thong before two fingers plunge into my wet core. I sigh with relief. My grinding becomes erratic, my moans intensify. I freefall and release my juices over Dirk's questing fingers.

"Fuck! You're so fucking wet," Dirk growls. My eyes clash with his. He pulls his hand from between my legs and places his wet fingers into his mouth. "Delicious," he proclaims, cleaning his fingers of my juices.

"Shit." Nikolai growls before lifting himself from the sofa. He sniffs the air making a loud sound with each inhale. "I get to feast on her pussy first," Nikolai says. Nikolai lifts me out of Dirk's clutches and takes me into his arms.

I look between the two when Dirk stands to his feet. Dirk has a cocky smirk on his face. "I think we should let the lady decide!" His right brow arches upwards with his words.

"Ahh— I—" my voice trails off when rapid knocking begins at the door.

"I know Kassidy's in there!" shouts Leelayna from the other side of the door.

"Yeah!" Anita's voice joins in. "Whoever you are, my friend better me in one piece."

"Open the fucking door this instant!" Octavia and my other friend's mutterings join in.

The sound of my friends' voices splashes me back into reality. Oh my God! What have I let these two men do to me? I have to get out of here. I sprint to the door and click the lock before Dirk's voice reaches my ears.

"You can't run from destiny, Kass."

"You are meant to be ours. Now that we have found you, we are never letting you go," Nikolai adds. The boldness from their words scare the hell out of me. I just need to get away from their great awareness before I submit to their proposed foolery.

"What's going on in here Kassidy?"

"Are you okay?"

"Do we need to call the police?"

"Fuck the police! Do we need to kick anybody's ass for hurting you? I took taekwondo when I was in high school." My friend's various voices greet me.

"Let's go. I just need to get out of here," I tell my friends.

Leelayna attempts to enter the room, but I push her back.

"I'll tell you all everything when we get in the car," I promise them.

The sound of footsteps sounds behind me. "Go!" I

shout and take off running like the boogeyman is chasing me. My friends follow close behind fussing along the way.

A ringing sound penetrates my sluggish state and I pop up in bed. Got damn it—it was all a dream!

CHAPTER THIRTEEN

Kassidy

I arrive to work the next morning with my dream heavily on my mind. The dream has me uneasy and I wish there was a way for me to avoid my two bosses today.

I barely speak to the security guy, Branson, when I enter the building. I punch the elevator and head straight for the cafeteria. Maybe the caffeine will wake me up, help me to think clearly, and get my emotions under control.

The cafeteria isn't too full, I am third in line so I should be able to get my coffee fairly quickly. The smell of bacon and eggs makes my belly growl, but I don't have time for food.

"Good morning beautiful," a voice says near my

ear. A shiver runs down my spine as a minty breath caresses my ear.

I turn to face my boss; my heart rate increases and I have to force a greeting past my lips.

"Ah, good morning, Mr. Hawkings," I reply as thoughts of my dream accelerate inside my head. I try to get my breathing under control because my breath comes in pants and I feel like I want to suddenly faint. My heart is hammering like mad inside my chest.

"You must call me Dirk, remember?" He touches the side of my cheek right there in the cafeteria for everyone to see. I instantly shy away from his touch.

"You had an eyelash on your cheek. Blow and make a wish," he tells me holding his finger up to my lips. My skin still tingles where Dirk touched me and my heart pounds erratically in my chest.

I close my eyes and do as he says; wishing that the floor would open up and swallow me because looking at Dirk only brings back memories of last night's dream.

"What did you wish?"

My eyes fly open, and I reply, "If I tell you my wish it won't come true."

"Try me, maybe I can help you to make your wish come true," Dirk's voice is low and sensuous.

Lord have mercy! I can't cope this early in the morning with all of his hotness, and my body wakes up under his come-hither stare. As shameful as it is to admit, I must do so. I find Dirk beyond gorgeous and sexy, and I want him. In a bad way.

"Next!" the cashier calls out.

"What are you getting?" Dirk asks me.

"A Vanilla Latte with extra foam."

"I got it," Dirk says stepping around me to the counter. He quickly orders my latte and a black coffee for himself.

"Thank you," I say when he gives me my drink.

"No, thank you for the tremendous job you're doing at N&D," he follows along beside me as I head out the cafeteria and to the bank of elevators that will take us to our floor.

"I have a confession to make," Dirk says once we are on the elevator alone.

"What is it?" I peek up at him before casting my eyes down to the elevator's floor.

"I waited for you to come into work and followed you to the cafeteria."

"Oh!" I feel a blush spread over my body from his confession. I don't know how to react with him not being his usual smart-ass domineering self.

"Why are you so nice to me all of a sudden?"

Dirk reaches over and presses an elevator button, and it comes to a halt. Before I know what's happening, he grabs me and pulls my body against his. I almost lose my hold on my cup, but right it just in time.

"What are you doing?"

"I'm going to do what I've been craving to do for the longest." Dirk bends, bringing his lips flush against my own. Dirk has one arm around my waist and lifts me slightly, so that he can better indulge in the kiss. I allow my lips to part for his delving tongue. He begins his exploration, and my senses start to explode. I moan and revel in his seduction. Suddenly, his grip loosens around my waist, and he sets me back on my feet.

"Fuck!" Dirk growls out his blue eyes blazing into mine.

"Ah," I attempt to speak, but I'm at a loss for words. I lick my lips still tasting his minty kiss on my mouth. Dirk follows the movement of my tongue with a dark look in his gaze.

"I didn't mean for that to happen, but I'm glad it did."

"You didn't?" I ask suddenly feeling shy.

"Kassidy, don't look at me like that. I will tear that skirt from your body and do to you what I've been fantasizing of doing to you." The look in Dirk's eyes tells me he's not kidding.

"But you said you didn't mean to kiss me."

"I didn't, but I couldn't help myself. Do you have

any idea how temptingly beautiful you are?" Dirk's question makes me blush.

"No," I answer honestly. "I don't think I'm ugly— I think I look alright. I'm nothing special."

"I think I'm going to have to help you change your perception," he says grabbing my free hand and placing it between his legs.

My hands cover a hard outline that feels like a small baseball bat. My eyes widen, and a gasp slips past my lips.

"Yeah, that's what you do to me." Dirk squeezes my hand on top of his covered shaft and lets out an animalistic growl.

He leans down and presses a soft kiss on my lips again before pressing hot kisses along my jawline and moving down to my neck. He nibbles me softly on my collar bone, making my nipples harden, and my panties become saturated. My breath hitches and Dirk lets out a low growl deep in his throat. He slides his tongue against mine, twirling it around. I can feel his hard shaft pushing against me, and we begin to move together, grinding our bodies against one another.

Dirk devours my mouth, muffling my sigh as it emerges from my lips. "Damn, I better stop," Dirk growls and pulls away from me again. "I—"

"There's no need to explain," I turn and hurriedly press the button for the elevator to start up again.

Desire cloaks us like mist in the elevator, but we both remain quiet until we reach our floor.

"Kassidy, I will finish what I started later, and that's a promise," Dirk tells me before getting off the elevator and heading towards his office.

I drop into my chair once I reach my desk and take a deep breath. I don't know how to feel about Dirk kissing me, making me feel like being with him is definitely going to happen and not only in my dreams. I really need to go home, crawl into bed, pull the covers over my head and hide away from my sensuous thoughts. Especially away from my two sexy ass bosses.

I decided to send both Nikolai and Dirk a quick email. Alerting them that I've come down sick and I will work from home. I realize I'm running from my emotions, but I can't handle another encounter with Dirk or even Nikolai today. I grab my belongings and fly out of the building as if the devil himself is on my heels.

CHAPTER FOURTEEN

Kassidy

I open my front door to allow my friend Anita in. I can't help it—I smile when I notice the two wine bottles in her hand.

"Hey, my friend. I thought we could use these after the week we had. How are you doing?"

"I'm confused. But get in here. I'm glad you could come. We haven't had a girls night of hanging out in a while." I take the wine bottles from Anita's hand and kick the door closed with my bare foot. "Make yourself at home. I'm going to get us a couple of glasses."

"Sounds like a plan. I'm gonna drop my overnight bag in the guest room."

"Cool," I say walking into the kitchen to retrieve two clear wine glasses from the cabinet.

"I'm ordering pizza!" I hear Anita call out from the living room. "Does it matter what toppings?"

"Anything you order is fine," I tell her walking back into the room to pour us some wine.

I plop down on the sofa while Anita places our order.

"Pizza will be here in twenty minutes," she informs me.

"Great," I sigh and take a long sip from my glass.

Anita picks up her glass and sits in the comfy chair across from me. "What's going on with you woman?"

"I'm a slut," I blurt out.

"Shut the fuck up! You are so not a slut!" Anita exclaims before I can elaborate. Anita stares at me with a severe expression on her pretty face. I expel a long breath before speaking again.

"I am definitely a slut Anita."

"Why do you say that Kass?" she asks as her perfectly arched brows furrow. She leans forward in her seat awaiting my answer.

"I'm a really horrible person. I'm falling in lust or love with my incredibly gorgeous bosses. They both seem to desire me too. What the hell am I going to do Nita?"

I know she won't judge me because Anita is the most upfront, no holds barred friend that I have. I know she will give it to me straight, whether I like what she says or not.

Anita's eyes widen for a moment. Then she surprises me by pouring us more wine before gulping her entire glass down before speaking again.

"You lucky hoe!" She falls back in her chair kicking up her legs while laughing. I stare at her for a minute, trying to figure out what's so funny. A knock on the door interrupts me before I can question her.

"That must be the pizza," I say getting up to grab a twenty from my handbag I had placed on a table near the door earlier. "Keep the change," I tell the delivery guy after paying for the twelve dollar pizza.

"Damn Kass, I wish I had your dilemma," Anita teases. I place the pizza box on the center table. Nita gets up and comes to sit on the sofa.

"Seriously, Anita! This is a serious matter," I say before walking into my small kitchen to grab two paper plates and a roll of paper towels. Anita has already dug into the cheesy pizza by the time I return.

"I'm sorry for laughing, but you caught me off guard. I thought you were sick or something. I am serious when I say I wish I had two sexy, young, viral men lusting over me. Damn woman! Do you know what that would do to my ego?"

"What am I going to do?" I ask, picking up a slice of pizza and taking a bite. My eyes closed and I let out a moan as the fragrant toppings, and a burst of buttery garlic hit my taste buds.

"Mario's makes the best pizza, don't they?" I nod my head in agreement before taking another bite. "To answer your question, you are a single, beautiful and smart woman. Do you really have deep feelings for both of these men, deep enough to give yourself to them?"

"What do you mean exactly about giving myself to them, Anita?"

"You already know what I mean Kass," Anita wiggles her eyebrows suggestively. "Fuck them both and enjoy every salacious moment of it— then tell me about it afterward," she chuckles.

I groaned, "Well, I have a confession, I already kissed Nikolai. Dirk walked in on us. I think I would have gone all the way if Dirk didn't interrupt us when he did."

"Oh my God! What did Dirk say? How did Nikolai take the interruption?"

I take a drink from my wine glass before answering. "Well, Dirk acted all brooding, and Nikolai was furious about the interruption. Dirk said he needs to see me in his office first thing Monday morning. Oh, and Dirk kissed me too. I hope he doesn't fire me."

"What? Damn, you have all the luck but trust me, honey, that man isn't going to fire you. It sounds like

Dirk is jealous and that's why he kissed you to stake a claim of his own. Whew!" Anita fans her face. "It's getting hot in here talking about your gorgeous hunks."

I feel a nervous flutter like feeling in my stomach as I contemplate my friend's words. I nibble on my bottom lip to try and calm my nerves. "I guess I will know my fate on Monday morning with Dirk. That man is so hard to read at times."

"Yes, you will! In the meantime, we will enjoy the rest of this weekend— so no more worrying. Everything will sort itself out, I guarantee it."

I chuckle and reply, "If only I had a tenth of your optimism."

"Let's finish off these two bottles of wine. I promise you'll have it by then," Anita gives me a saucy wink and refills our glasses with the fruity wine. I laugh and nudge her shoulder with mine.

"Okay, bring it on!"

"What did I tell you?" Anita's voice is unusually loud in my ears. We had just finished up the last of the wine after some lighter conversation. "No worries right?"

"You're right. I'll be feeling absolutely no pain or stress," I nod in agreement.

"Of course you're not. Now let's watch a good movie on Netflix!" Anita suggests, jumping up from the couch to grab the remote. Watching movies is something we both like to do whenever we get together for a friend's night together.

Since I have a nice buzz going, I sit back to enjoy the rest of my weekend. Thoughts of seeing my handsome bosses can wait. I have until Monday to allow worry to invade my thoughts again.

The next day being Sunday, Anita and I both slept in late before getting up and going out for a late brunch at the Sweet Skillet, one of our favorite places to eat. We each devoured Belgian waffles topped with Nutella, softly scrambled eggs and Canadian bacon. After brunch, we hit the Fremont Sunday Street Market, to walk off the calories from our large brunch. We spent most of the afternoon shopping until early evening, and we gave each other a hug and said our goodbyes before heading home. I am tired by the time I enter my apartment, so after kicking off my flats in the bedroom, I place my shopping bags in my closet, promising myself to hang up the two blouses and skirts I bought later.

I really need a hot shower and then definitely bed. I peel off my clothes piece by piece on my way to the bathroom, leaving a trail on the floor. *I will pick them up later*, I think to myself as I turn on the shower making sure it's the right temperature. Sighing in satisfaction, I quickly wash before drying off, applying lotion to my damp skin and slipping into a nightshirt and a pair of white cotton panties. There is nothing like sleeping in a comfortable pair of underwear. I brush my teeth, floss and rinse my mouth with a minty mouthwash before heading to bed.

Although I'm exhausted, I find it hard to sleep. I peer at my alarm clock and notice it's a little past ten p.m. My cell phone chimes with an incoming message. I gaze at the dim screen and swipe to read the text of an unknown number.

This is Dirk, and this is my personal cell number. Save it and be on time tomorrow.

That was a short, bossy and direct message, I think to myself saving the number like I was told. I power off my phone, not even responding to Dirk's text. Maybe next time he will show better manners like *"Hello Kassidy this is Dirk. Please don't forget to be on time tomorrow,"* but no! His message has to border on being rude. *Forget Dirk Hawkings!* I need to get some sleep. I close my eyes and slowly count backward from one hundred...

"Wake up sweetheart," a gruff voice whispered in my ear. I feel a soft nip at my earlobe before a warm tongue swirls around the rim of my ear.

"Mmm", I let loose a lustful sigh.

"You have on too many clothes," the deep husky voice continues. I attempt to raise my eyes but they are heavy, and I feel drunk on desire. My eyes remain closed for the moment.

Suddenly, I feel hot and flushed all over. I can feel my nightshirt and panties dissipating from my body, piece by piece. I find myself enveloped in a pair of strong, muscular arms. At the same time, I feel my legs being pried apart by another set of hands just as a different voice says, "I want to taste you." A hot tongue instantly starts lapping at the seam of my slick entrance.

"Ahh," I cry out in pleasure when I feel my breasts being squeezed and my nipples being sucked on at the same time a tongue plunges into my pussy. Waves of desire wash over my entire frame causing me to squirm in intense pleasure.

"Your pussy is so sweet. I can feast on your nectar forever," a voice murmurs against my wet sex. His tongue swipes back and forth before he sucks my clit into his mouth. I can feel the beginning of an orgasm building.

Impulsively, my hands grab the head between my legs, my fingers clutch silken strands of hair as I grind against his face. The squeezes and licks intensified at my breasts. I moan at the double sensations at my pussy and breasts. *My nipples are sensitive and feel hard as twin pebbles.*

"I'm cumming!" I cry out and my eyes fly open.

"Fuck, yeah, cum for us beloved," a deep, familiar voice caresses my ear. I look over, and my eyes collide with the silvery gaze of Nikolai.

"Do you like that sweetheart?" the other familiar voice grates out between my thighs. I force my gaze away from Nikolai to peer down between my legs. Dirk raises his head and his piercing blue gaze locks on mine. His lips are wet with my essence.

Dirk's large hand reaches for mine and slowly guides my fingers in between my slippery plump foals. He rubs my clit between his fingers, and I cry out in pleasure. Dirk slides his hand over mine and forces me to finger myself.

I moan in response to the pleasurable sensation between my thighs—a mix of sensuously exquisite desire zaps through me.

"Oh my God!" I gasp, turning my head towards Nikolai, nuzzling my face against his chest. I love the way my two lovers sandwich me in.

I luxuriate in two pairs of warm, wet lips kissing me all over my body, leaving no skin untouched.

Finally, Dirk rises and his lips meet mine with such urgency and hotness. I can feel a jolt of electricity sizzle through my entire body. I let out an involuntary moan and began grinding back and forth against Nikolai's fingers in a fit of uncontrolled desire.

I can feel a grin form on Dirk's lips, and he let out a primitive groan. "Oh, Kassidy, you're so fucking beautiful."

"You are ours, and we both adore you. There is nothing we wouldn't do for you and to you to make you happy, my love," Nikolai kisses my back and squeezes my ass cheeks. I feel his finger flit close to my rectum. Their words make me feel loved and cherished. Butterflies flutter around inside my belly. Dirk and Nikolai's fingers join at my wet sex and plunge their fingers deep thrusting in and out, out and in.

"Oh Nikolai and Dirk," I moan. "I need to feel you inside of me. Both of you." I cry out not caring how wanton I sound.

"Fuck," Dirk grunts. "I'm hard as granite."

"I want your cock in my mouth Dirk, and I want you to fill my pussy Nikolai," I whisper.

"You're soon going to have your wish," Dirk says gruffly, his breathing sounds raspy. Their fingers pull out my wet sex, and I moan.

"Don't worry sweetheart. You will be filled with both of our cocks soon enough," Nikolai says, bringing his nectar coated wet fingers up to my lips and sliding them into my mouth. "Do you see how sweet you taste?" he growls.

I nod while sucking my juices clean from his fingers. Dirk nudges his fingers inside my mouth and says, "Suck," after Nikolai removes his fingers. I waste no time in sucking my essence from his fingers as well.

"Oh, shit," Dirk groans, placing his mouth on mine, to get a taste of my nectar on my lips. "Are you ready for my cock?"

"Mmm," I moan my consent. Dirk pulls me closer by my waist and directs me to kneel in front of him with my ass up in the air. They both hurry out the rest of their clothes and come back to me. Dirk's erection is in direct alignment with my mouth. Nikolai spreads my thighs and places his hard length at my wet entrance from the back.

My mouth starts to water at the thought of taking Dirk's hard length in between my lips—and Nikolai's inside my wet pussy. My tongue swipes against the swollen head of Dirk's massive cock, causing him to suck in a breath. I lick at the tip of his swollen head, running my wet tongue over the surface slowly.

"Mmm. You're fucking killing me," Dirk groans. He shoves his length down my throat at the same time Nikolai plunges deep inside my wet pussy. I gag and moan at the same time. Finally, I'm claimed by both of the men that I'd desired from the first moment I laid eyes on them

This is everything I've craved and so much more. I

want Dirk and Nikolai more than anything I've ever wanted before. I need these men like I need air to breathe. I breathe in Dirk's scent and suck harder. I can taste his precum, and I want him to give everything to me.

Nikolai wraps his arms around my waist as his thrusts pick up the pace. I push back, stroke for stroke as he pleasures my throbbing pussy.

In one swift motion, Nikolai pushes inside my heat to the hilt. He's silently demanding his place in my heart and body. Both of these men mean so much to me. I could never choose between the two.

Nikolai bends and places his lips at the base of my damp neckline. I moan and push my hips back hard against his hard steel cock, grinding my slick pussy up and down his erection.

"Fuck— fuck— fuck!" Nikolai growls behind me and shoots his load deep inside my dripping wet pussy.

Dirk growls and releases his hot seed down my throat at the same time my nectar sprays Nikolai's cock.

A piercing noise awakes me, and I jump up in bed. *Damn!* I scream disappointed that I'm in bed alone, and it's Monday morning! Now it's time for me to get to work. *Another damn dream!*

~

MONDAY MORNING

I place my handbag in my desk drawer, power on my computer, and get to work. I make sure to check my emails first. I have an email from Nikolai informing me to come straight to his office. I walk the short distance to Nikolai's office and tap lightly on his door before entering. He is on the telephone but he beckons me to take a seat.

I watch him and can't seem to take my eyes off Nikolai who is dressed in a navy blue custom made suit. The fit of the material across his broad shoulders causes me to cross one leg over the other and squeeze, trying my best to assuage the throbbing in my inner core.

My breath hitches in my throat when our gazes clash. Nikolai's gaze glazes over my face down to the plush display of cleavage teasing out the top of my scooped neckline blouse.

I breathe again when Nikolai suddenly swivels his chair around to face the set of picturesque windows leaving his back to me. I notice the sheen of his light colored hair that's tied back with a hair tie. I wonder how warm and smooth it feels to the touch.

"That will have to do for now, but trust me, the final decision lies with N&D," Nikolai's voice is curt as he ends the call.

Suddenly, he swivels back around facing me. He stands, approaches me and comes to stand in front of the chair I'm sitting in.

"Kassidy," he says with a warm undertone. "I'm sorry for keeping you waiting."

I gaze up into Nikolai's light gray eyes, my nipples harden from the way he's looking at me. I uncross my legs and smooth the soft material of my skirt down when I feel his eyes on my upper thighs.

"No problem. Ah, what did you want to see me about?" I ask.

"Would you like something to drink—coffee or water perhaps?" Nikolai asks.

"No, thank you," I reply.

Nikolai leans back against his desk and crosses his arms across his muscular chest while staring into my eyes.

I begin to fidget in my seat and cross my legs again. Heat flares up in Nikolai's eyes and his nostrils flare wide.

"Are you nervous Kassidy?" he asks. A smirk appears around his mouth with the question.

I nibble the inside of my bottle lip until I taste copper. *Welp, this is it. I'm fired.*

"Do I have anything to be nervous about?" I ask. "I'm sorry I left early last Friday, but I really wasn't feeling well. I..."

"No, you don't have anything to be nervous about."

I breathed out a long breath of relief.

Nikolai grinned. "Kassidy, I have a proposition for you. This has nothing to do with your job. You can say no without fear of losing your position here at N&D."

My heartrate kicked up a notch. "I'm curious," I reply. "What is your proposition?"

I still have a job... that's the news I held on to with growing happiness. Anything else I could handle. Maybe Nikolai needed me to work extra hours. I wouldn't have any problems with that. I had no one to worry about at home anyway. I was no one's wife or mother. *No one's girlfriend either*, I thought with sadness.

Nikola's voice brought me out of my musings.

"I'm sorry, what did you say?"

Nikolai scowled, and I gave him an apologetic look. I sat up in the chair straighter and gave him my undivided attention.

"I said that I want to apologize for how brusque Dirk has been around you. He's not usually so ill tempered. The thing is, we both find you extremely sexy and lovely. As I said before, while this is not a requirement to the job, we want you to enter into an intimate relationship with us. Of course, there certainly would be many perks to entering a relationship with both of us if you decide to."

Both of them! Did Nikolai just ask me to enter into an intimate relationship with him and Dirk?

I must be dreaming because nothing like this could ever happen to a woman like me. Dreams and fantasies aside, this couldn't be real. I curled my fingers inwardly and dug my nails into the palms of my hands. Sharp pain pierced through my flesh.

Nope! I wasn't dreaming. I was very much awake and sitting before Nikolai in his office.

"Do you have anything to say?" Nikolai asked regarding me with a serious stare.

"Ah, I don't know what to say," I reply with my heart hammering against my chest. Suddenly I feel faint, and butterflies are flitting around my belly.

"Are you alright Kassidy? Here take this bottle of water," Nikolai says pushing the opened water bottle into my hand.

I don't even remember him walking over to the small refrigerator in a corner behind his desk. My thoughts are all over the place. I need to talk to Anita ASAP.

I whispered a thank you and swallowed half of the contents in the bottle. Something stronger would be better in times like this.

"Are you better now?" Nikolai asks.

I bob my head up and down before replying, "Yes."

"Take some time and think about it, and sleep on it. You can give me your answer on tomorrow."

"Okay," I nod and stand to my feet on jittery legs. "Will that be all for now?"

"Yes, but are you sure you're alright? I know I sprung this—"

"Don't worry about me, I'm sure I'll be fine once I think things over."

Nikolai gave me a warm glance as he pushed off the desk and invaded my space. His cologne penetrated my nostrils and I automatically leaned into him, "Are you positive, you're okay?" His hands settled on my waist

I nodded again. "I need to get to work."

Nikolai's hands slid from my waist. One hand briefly caressed my cheek. He takes one of my hands in his and walks me to the door.

"I will await your answer with patience until tomorrow."

"Alright," I nod, gazing up into his piercing stare.

Nikolai leans forward as if he wants to kiss me. My eyes shutter closed, my lips part slightly.

"I'll see you later Kassidy," Nikolai says. My eyes fly open, he grins, and takes a step back, closing the door gently behind him.

I stand there lost in my thoughts for a few seconds before making my way back to my desk.

CHAPTER FIFTEEN

Dirk

I glance up from the papers spread across my desk and think about Kassidy and how the talk went with Nikolai. We had both decided it was best for him to approach Kassidy with our proposal. I didn't want to scare her away, knowing that Nikolai would have the smoother delivery in our appeal to win her over.

A fierce need shimmers through me at the thought of having Kassidy in our bed. She is the one. The woman that is made for the both of us.

I clamp my fist around the shaft of the black sleek pen as my shaft pulses to life with all the delectable things I want to do to Kassidy's voluptuous body. Maybe I need to hit the gym to work out some of my sexual frustrations. Now that Kassidy has entered my life, no other woman will do.

Maybe I should just call it a day. It is after hours, but I'm still sitting here at N&D with Kassidy heavily on my mind. I shuffle the papers I'm working on back into a neat pile and decide to call it a day.

I power down the computer, grab my messenger bag, and head out the door. I could stop by the lounge tonight, but I wasn't in the mood to even be around other people right now. Well, that's with the exception of Kassidy. My temper is quick, and my irritation levels are up all because I need to fuck Kassidy and make a claim. But tonight I worked later than normal trying to smother my desire for Kassidy through my work.

I bid the Security Guard good night as I left the building and got into my vehicle. Soon, I pull into my driveway and into the double door garage. I expel a long frustrated breath, as I let myself into my home and disarm the beeping alarm, with the security code.

I wonder how it would feel coming home to Kassidy? Being alone never bothered me before meeting her. I almost let my stubborn nature make me miss out on what I already knew in my heart to be true.

I am in love with Kassidy and had fallen for her the moment I saw her walk into my office. I know the same is true for Nikolai.

I walk into the kitchen and place my bag down by

the kitchen door. I shrug off my suit jacket and place it over a kitchen chair before making my way over to the sink to wash my hands. Walking over to the refrigerator, I open the door and take out leftovers from the Chinese restaurant. I pull out a carton of beef and vegetables, and egg rolls before making my way over to the microwave to warm it up.

Eating alone would be a thing of the past soon. Nikolai and I would make sure of it. Sitting down at the table, I dug into my reheated meal with relish. Just the thought of Kassidy inhabiting my home, or one we built together, makes me anxious.

After eating, I walk upstairs to the bedroom, shower and brush my teeth. I wished that Kassidy was here to join me, I thought as I slid between the cool sheets of my King-sized bed.

That woman is ingrained into my every thought and dream.

It's my own damn fault that Kassidy isn't in my bed right now. The voice inside my head scolded me. I knew that I couldn't beat myself up over my past mistakes, but I must move forward and play it smart if I wanted to woo Kassidy to Nikolai's and my way of thinking.

I really need to get some sleep if I wanted to be on my A-game on tomorrow. I had a mission...

Woo Kassidy, fuck Kassidy, and never let her go. I

clicked off my bedside lamp and closed my eyes on those thoughts.

∽

Kassidy

THE NEXT DAY

"Did you need to see me?" I ask Nikolai as he sits behind his desk.

His eyes meet mine and my panties saturate on the spot. I swear Nikolai gets sexier every time I see him.

"Do you have an answer for me?" Nikolai asks getting straight to the point.

My heart hammers against my chest. I didn't think Nikolai would push me for an answer this soon in the day. I hoped he would at least give me to the end of my shift. He pushes back his chair and stands to his feet. I stand straighter and smooth my hair, which I have in a low bun.

"Ahh, I--" my words become stuck in my throat as Nikolai walks towards me.

Nikolai's gaze is fiery as his eyes rake over my body.

"God, you're so beautiful," he says crowding my space. I can't help but to inhale his cologne. He always smells too damn good for me to think rationally.

"Did you want..." I stop my words mid-sentence when his hand reaches out to caress my face. It's obvious my thoughts flee me whenever he gets too close.

"I need for you to say yes to my question. Maybe this will help you with your decision," Nikolai says, gripping my waist and pulling me closer. His head descends, and my eyes flutter shut.

Nikolai kisses me passionately and deeply.

I can feel the prodding of his erection against my belly, and a moan escapes my lips. The sexual energy between us soars to new heights. Suddenly, I feel his hands rake over my full breasts which makes my nipples stand to immediate attention. Nikolai squeezes my supple breasts and cup them into his hands.

I cry out when he pinches my covered nipples and rolls them between his fingers. His bold manipulations causes jolts of pleasure to shoot straight to my core.

One of my hands presses against Nikolai's chest. I don't know whether I want to pull him closer or push him away. I need to gather my focus and really think about my bosses' proposal before giving them an answer.

Besides, did Dirk really want this? He had been treating me like shit lately. Maybe Nikolai got it wrong. Maybe--

"Touch me," Nikolai growls as he takes my hand

and places it against his massive erection. I let out a whine, and happily encircle part of his shaft. His erection is too big for my fingers to meet.

A mixture of excitement and fear grows within me at the thought of touching him bare. It's as if Nikolai reads my thoughts. He mutters against my lips, "Unzip me and take me into your hands."

Without missing a beat, I do as Nikolai instructs. I reach inside his boxers to grasp at his thick, hard shaft. I brush my hand up and down its smooth, satiny length. His huge cock is hot and pulsing in my hand, and I just want to feel it deep inside my slick heat.

I cry out when Nikolai pushes up my blouse along with my black lace bra and takes one of my nipples into his hot mouth. Electrical chills of pleasure slide all over my body. I give Nikolai's cock a hard squeeze, and he growls out my name against his sensual lips. His thick cock is rock hard, and it feels so good in my palm of my hands.

Am I really going to allow Nikolai to have me in his office?

"Be ours—say yes. I won't take no for an answer," Nikolai says through more passionate kisses.

"Yes! I will be yours and Dirk's!" I cry out.

Nikolai pushes me backwards against his desk and proceeds to take my shirt off. He sits me on the edge of the desk and my mind screams for me to stop him.

What if someone walks in? I become nervous at the thought and voice my concerns to Nikolai.

"Someone may walk in," I barely get out of my mouth.

Nikolai mutters, "But that's half the fun," and goes back to kissing me like he's on a mission.

~

LATER THAT EVENING

I pick up my drink and take a sip. "Anita, what am I gonna do? I told Nikolai earlier today that I would have a relationship with him and Dirk. What the hell have I committed to?"

"You are lucky, honey! I wish I had your concerns. I would think I'd died and gone to heaven. You better handle that situation and handle it well," my friend suggests.

Maybe my friend is right. I accepted the proposal, so I shouldn't doubt it.

"Thank you for always listening to me," I say.

"Honey, stop overthinking your decision." Anita reaches across the table and gives my hand a reassuring pat.

Frown lines still burrow between my brows. I can't still wonder did I make the right choice. I have never had to contemplate a decision of this magnitude in my entire life.

"Let's change the subject for a while. We need to do something special for your upcoming birthday."

Yeah, my thirty-third birthday was coming up in a few weeks. I sigh inwardly. Another birthday I crave without any big party or fanfare. Staying home ordering pizza, watching a good movie, and eating junk food was good enough for me.

"I think I'd rather stay in and do our usual," I tell my friend.

"No way! Don't worry about it, I'll come up with an idea that will make you happy. Do you trust me?"

"You know I do. I just don't like making a big deal out of me turning another year older."

Anita gives me a look. "Honey, don't you know that getting older is to be celebrated?"

"You're right," I reply.

"Damn straight I'm right," Anita grins. "Now tell me who do you want invited to this shindig?" Anita's eyes are full of excitement. "I already know you want your two sexy bosses to be there, so that's a given."

I take a quick sip from my drink. "I'm not sure it's a good idea to invite them. I was thinking even if we go out, we could make it a girls night out."

"We will see. Just leave everything to me," Anita replies with a twinkle in her gaze.

"Anita--"

"Hush up and finish your drink," she says cutting me off.

I blow out a breath of frustration. When Anita set her mind to something, there is no use of me trying to change it, even if the circumstances have to do with me.

Anita and I have light banter and laughs for the rest of our stay at the bar. We parted ways on exiting the building with the promise of calling each other soon.

Later that night, I walk into my apartment feeling more than a little tipsy. Right now, I am feeling no pain and don't have a care in the world. Shedding my clothes, I pull back the bedcovers in my bedroom and face plant right in the middle of my bed. I know without a doubt I would sleep like a new born babe.

CHAPTER SIXTEEN

Kassidy

A FEW DAYS LATER

"Dirk, may I ask you a question?"

"Sure, what's up?" Dirk's voice is low but filled with sensual sexiness instead of his usual sarcasm of the past. His usual response before I agreed to be his and Nikolai's woman would have been something like, "*Get on with it, Kassidy. We have work to do.*"

Then I would have said something like, "*You don't have to be such an ass about it.*"

I glance down, at the notepad in my hand. I really don't know how to handle this new, charismatic, and kindhearted Dirk without the glare and harsh words.

"Why were you mean to me in the past, and are you really on board with Nikolai's proposal?"

A low growl comes from Dirk's chest and I jump in surprise.

"Of course I am. What makes you question it?"

"Since I have never been anything but courteous with you and—"

My words catches in my throat when Dirk looks up from the file he has lying open on his desk. His hot gaze plunges into mine. His eyes slowly rake over me from head to toe. His slow perusal of me starts a flame simmering in the pit of my stomach. Slowly, it spreads to my feminine core. I squeeze my thighs together to assuage my throbbing clit.

"Most times, you didn't even pay me any attention. You showed noting but dislike for me," I add before I lose my nerves.

Dirk prop his foot on the edge of his desk. "I'm sorry. I can be an ass most times. I was wrong for treating you wrongly. I hope you can find it in your heart to forgive me for my crass conduct."

"You know at one time I thought you disliked me because I'm older than the majority of your employees."

"Do you want me to prove you wrong, Kassidy?" He leans back in his seat. A fire seems to be lurking in the depths of his heated stare.

"I didn't know what to think, you know." I lick my lips that have suddenly gone dry. "Your behavior had me baffled more times than I want to remember."

"I guess I was jealous. I still am, I suppose, but it depends on how you answer my question. "Do you find Nikolai more attractive than me? Don't lie. I've seen the way you watch him. And I've seen the cold look in your eyes whenever you glanced my way."

"We are at work. You and Nikolai are my bosses and I don't think this conversation is appropriate for the workplace."

"Fucking you isn't appropriate either, but that's all I've been thinking of doing since the first moment I laid eyes on you."

My eyes widen in surprise. I muddle inwardly over my words before I speak. "Um, you sure fooled me. You acted like you hated me most times."

I can feel a slow burn simmering in my belly from Dirk's admission. I don't want him to know how affected I am by his words.

"Again sweetheart, I'm sorry. I don't hate you, Kass. Far from it. I really want to taste your lips." His gaze latches on to my mouth.

"What did you just say?" I ask as Dirk moves his gaze away from my lips and his sexy gaze plunges back into mine.

Emotion stirs inside my frame. Suddenly, I don't know what to do with myself.

"Do you want me to kiss you Kassidy?" he asks, with a one-sided grin attached to his kissable lips. "Do you want me to show you how sorry I am, baby?"

Is this some type of joke? Are Nikolai and Dirk going to pass me between them in the office like this? Even though all I did was make out heavily with Nikolai, would making out behind Nikolai's back be within the rules? How is thing between us going to work?

"I don't think it would be professional to start something in the office. I'm not some immature—"

"I take you for a classy, mature woman who knows what she wants out of life. You're smart, you work hard, and you're beautiful. You're the kind of woman I need to keep me in line. You aren't afraid to say what's on your mind. I like that trait in a woman. Hell! I really like you," Dirk presses a button on his desk, I hear the blinds closing, and then the lock on the office door clicks into place.

Suddenly, we are enclosed in Dirk's office from prying eyes. Alone. My heart starts to beat faster in my chest. The palms of my hands become sweaty.

"What are you doing?" my eyes widen as he pushes back his seat, stands, and strolls around his desk to stand in front of me. My eyes automatically settle on his crotch area. I gasp and gulp when I notice the impressive bulge beneath his slacks.

"Fuck!" Dirk growls out, and my eyes snap up to his face.

Busted! I flush when I see the look of fire in his eyes. He knows I was checking out his erection. Damn, it *was* just there. How could I ignore it?

I follow his movement as if in slow motion. Dirk's fingers rake through his long hair. The way he's staring down at me-- it's sexy as hell, and it makes my pussy pulse with need. I wonder what his tanned skin would feel like under his shirt. I secretly crave to touch Dirk's tall, muscled frame. His broad shoulders stretch the material of his shirt to perfection.

"I don't know what you want from me. I'm not into--"

"Into what?" Dirk inches closer to me. He leans down, places his hands on the armrests of the chair I'm sitting in. "Kiss me," Dirk grunts.

Desire course through my body from his words.

The notepad and pen drop listlessly from my hand to the floor. My voice deserts me at that moment in time. I turn my head twice in the negative silently saying *no*.

"Yes, you shouldn't say no to my kisses..." he says pulling me to my feet as he stands to his full height. "I wonder what your kisses taste like. I wonder what your pussy must taste like. Those thoughts plague me day and night since I met you. It kills me to be around you and not touching you. Do you have any idea what you do to me, Kassidy?"

"I make you treat me like your office plaything?" I question him, feeling confused as he hauls me against his chest.

"Hell no, you're no one's plaything. I've been a dick. It won't happen again. I promise."

Dirk's head bends, I close my eyes, breathe in his spicy cologne when his mouth crushes against mine.

Dirk's lips feel soft and gentle against mine. His lips are sensual and exploring. His tongue pushes inside my mouth making me gasp, and he wraps his tongue around my tongue and sucks. My panties become wetter. I become hotter.

A moan builds and eases from my throat; my arms wrap around Dirk's toned waist. My fingers go to work stroking his back. Dirk deepens the kiss; my legs become like jelly. I am weak.

My mouth opens wider to receive his thrusting tongue, and I desire to savor this moment for a lifetime. It may not ever happen again. So I better enjoy it while I can.

"Mm, just as I thought, your mouth tastes delicious," Dirk grunts.

My nipples harden. My breasts ache to be touched and squeezed.

I whimper as my hands ease up to his broad shoulders. I press my chest closer to his body. Dirk lets out an animalistic groan. His hand finds one covered breast, he gives it a deliberate squeeze before fondling a pebbled nipple.

"Oh yes," I moan and he caresses my other breast, giving it the same attention.

Dirk lifts his head breaking our heated kiss. I breathe in a fortifying breath feeling at a loss.

"I want more," he says. "I want to taste all of you. Be inside you. Please tell me that you want the same sweetheart."

"I do," I whisper noting the desire on the hard planes of his handsome face, and in the glint of his lust filled gaze. I can't believe this man desires me, as much as I want him.

Dirk presses firmly against me, and I can certainly feel the prominent proof in the hard thrust of his erection against my stomach.

Lust in his eyes intensifies as he holds my gaze. "I'm going to make love to you Kassidy." My eyes travel over to his chest area. I need a reprieve for the look in his stare is burning me alive. "Look at me, sweetheart."

The muscles in Dirk's jawline are clenching. It's as if he's fighting for control.

I nod my head up and down.

"I need to hear you say it, Kassidy. Do you want me to make love to you?" Tiny butterflies flit inside my belly. I crave this man standing before me like my next breath. But if I were, to be honest, I feel the exact same way about Nikolai. Am I going insane? How can this be? An overwhelming feeling courses through my body. I can't do this; I know this is wrong on so many levels. I take a step back. Dirk follows. He takes my hand in his, brings it to his mouth and places a soft kiss in the palm of my hand.

"My job-- I don't want to jeopardize--"

"I swear to you, your job here is safe. This is about you and me. I need you, Kassidy. I need my mate."

"I need you too, and I want you to make love to me," I reply letting go of my doubts. I slide a hand over the stubble that lines his jaw. The desire in his eyes reflects my own.

Wait, did he call me his mate? Is that a new word I missed for girlfriend or something?

"Mine." Dirk grunts holding me in a tight grip. "I want to make love to you. Right now," he mutters.

My hand continues to flit against his jawline. "I want you to make love to me. Now." The hesitation has vanished. Damn the repercussions. I want this. I desire Dirk.

Dirk helps me strip out of my clothes. "Keep your heels on," Dirk directs.

"Okay," I whisper my consent as he reaches around to unsnap my pink lacy bra. My bountiful breasts spill into his hands when he tosses the bra aside.

"You're perfect," he says. "I could feast on these forever," he adds as he unzips my skirt. It puddles at my feet. He bends to help me step out of it before removing my matching pink panties.

He throw aside my skirt. I suck in the softness of my belly when he places a light kiss near my navel.

Need and desire run rampant through my system. I've never felt this type of consuming emotion when I was with Stanley. Stanley was never big on foreplay or cared for me getting an orgasm. I always had to take care of myself when he fell asleep. But with Dirk it's different. I feel like I can come from just kissing him.

I love this intense feeling of chemistry between the two of us. My body craves to be taken. To be caught up and forget my need to remain levelheaded.

Dirk's mouth clamps down on mine. His teeth nip at my lips, becoming teasing just before his thrusting tongue claims mine.

"Take your clothes off—" I gasp against his mouth.

Dirk grunts, steps away from me, and began shrugging off his clothes. God-- this man's body is chiseled to perfection. My hand itches to caress every inch of him.

151

Soon, Dirk is standing before me taking my breasts in his hand. He squeezes and plucks my dark pebbled nipples with his fingers. Electrical shocks run straight to my feminine core.

I arch my back to get closer to him. My breath comes out in spurts from pleasure. Dirk's massive cock taps with impatience against my stomach.

My pussy juices drip down the inside of my thighs from my wantonness. I shiver when Dirk's hand sweeps over the curve of my hip.

"Mm, I need you, Dirk. I want you inside me. Please tell me you have protection."

"Yeah...but I want to taste you first."

Oh God! I silently scream inside my head.

Dirk's hands caress up and down my body. Slowly he inches down to the wet heat between my thighs.

"Dirk!"

He explores my moist, plump lips. Ever so gently, he touches the heated flesh of my pussy. But I begin arching against his caress, his touch becomes bolder when he pushes two fingers into my core.

Dirk bends his head taking a nipple between his lips. I tremble at the contact of his tongue licking my sensitive nipple.

"Condom," I hiss and reach for his massive erection.

Dirk pulls away, evading my touch. "If you touch

me right now, I may not last," he confesses. I watch him with desire filled eyes. He reaches down for his slacks and retrieves a condom from the pocket. He tears the packet open with his straight white teeth and rolls it on his hard length.

He grabs me and leads me over to a comfortable looking sofa in the office. "Sit."

I sit, and he comes down before me on his knees. He cups both of my brown globes in his big hands, squeezing my breasts together, he licks both nipples at the same time.

Dirk sucks my nipples so hard it borders on pain, but the harder he sucks the wetter I become.

Dirk slides his hand between the junction of my thighs and more nectar gathers between my slick folds.

His lips find a path across my stomach area, and his other hand drapes one of my legs over his shoulder. He blows ever so softly over my slick nub, and my hands find their way to his silken hair. His strands feel electric to my fingers.

Dirk swipes his tongue up and down the length of my core and then his hot tongue dives into me and French kisses my pussy.

"Mm," I cry out and undulate my hips with the tempo of his tongue lashings. I can feel my orgasm bubbling to the forefront.

"Come for me Kassidy," Dirk orders me, and I arch

my back, crying out my pleasure falling over a cliff of blissfulness.

My entire frame is trembling with the aftermath of my pleasure. Dirk gives me one last swipe with his tongue before easing to his feet. He places me on the couch to his liking then drapes his lithe body over mine to dive his latex covered shaft deep into my core.

"Ahhh," I sigh as my inside wraps tightly around his length. I feel pleasure and a pinch of pain from his length and girth.

"Are you okay sweetheart?" Dirk pulls back to look down at me with concern in his eyes.

"I'm more than okay," I half gasp when he starts to move slowly inside my heat.

"Do you know how long I've wanted to do this? To be inside you— loving you like this?"

"Please make love to me," I moan. "Dirk, I need you so much!"

Dirk eases his hardness out of me before plunging balls deep into my wet sex. He's holding himself up by his elbows, so he's able to maintain eye contact with each delicious thrust.

"Do you like that?" he grunts and swivels his hips on a downward thrust.

"Yes!" I cry out not caring who hears me as he repeatedly plunges into my warmth. My hips rise to match his rhythm. Dirk's grunts add to my moans as his cock sank into me faster and faster. I wrap my legs around his trim waist and hold on for the ride.

"Ahh, Dirk!" I cry out when he pulls out of me. He stands and grabs my hand leading me over to his desk.

"Plant your hands firmly on the desk, spread your legs and push your butt out," he tells me. I have no qualms about doing what he directed.

I bite my bottom lip when I feel his cock prying at my entrance.

"You're damn tight," Dirk grunts into my ear as his body leans into mine. I tremble. "Are you still okay?" he asks.

"I feel only pleasure," I assure him. Dirk kisses my shoulder, and I give a start when his teeth bite down into the flesh.

My head turns and meets his gaze. "Mine, all mine," he grunts and at that moment I can't deny it. I'm all his.

His lips immediately assuage his love bite. "Mm," I moan again and then jerk as if an electrical shock hits me when his hand slides over to cup my breast and squeezes.

"I love your breasts," he says fondling my nipples. "I also love this tight pussy," he states moving his hand down between my open thighs to stroke my sensitive clit. I feel as if I'm caught in a vortex and cry out when he plunges inside me to the hilt.

"Mm-mm- mmm," I moan as he drives into me with plummeting hard thrusts. Dirk continuously rubs my clit with each plunging thrust. "I'm coming," I whine as another release forces its way through my body.

"Shit," Dirk growl. "I'm coming."

I croon as the jerk of his cock causes spasms inside my core. Dirk surges into me one last time before coming to a halt. I can feel his sweat and heated breath on my back. All I want to do is curl up in his arms for the rest of the day and night. But reality comes back to me when I realize I just fucked my boss in his office while I'm on the clock.

Damn. Damn, damn!

"I wasn't too hard on you, was I?" Dirk says pulling away from me to dispose of the condom.

I shake my head.

"Answer me, Kassidy."

"No, you were just right," I look away from Dirk and hurriedly gather my clothes.

"Do you forgive me now?"

"Yes Dirk you're forgiven," I reply softly.

"Good." He gives me a simmering glance. I begin to heat up all over again. "You can use the restroom over there to freshen up if you like," he points.

"Thanks that would be great." I feel shame come over me for what I allowed to happen. *What the fuck is wrong with me?* I think as I huddle in the bathroom. I take wet wipes to wipe myself down in a hurry and put on my clothes, run my fingers through my hair and pat it down. *This will have to do.*

I open the bathroom door and find the office empty. Thank God. Dirk didn't want to face me either. Fine with me. I open the office door to head out and come face to face with Nikolai. I tremble in my bones when I see the look of rage attached to his handsome face.

He walks away before I can open my mouth to speak.

I walk over to a chair and sit down. I gasp as understanding and the truth dawns on me. At one time in life in my not so distant past, I questioned what it meant to have someone to truly love me.

I even wondered if I deserved love. I almost let myself fall victim to my own negative thinking of who I am as a woman. I recently realized I mustn't allow fear of the past to stop me from believing in love again— thinking that I'm not worthy of being loved.

I have to risk my heart, even knowing that it may be broken— again. I've learned that I can't see inside someone's soul or into their heart, but I must trust my instincts. I must explore all avenues of the beauty of love. Even with my flaws, vulnerabilities, and short-comings — I am lovable. I love myself, and I'm ready to step out of my comfort zone. I admit I'm scared, but I have faith that I'm ready. More than prepared to begin again.

CHAPTER SEVENTEEN

Nikolai

"Good morning Nikolai," Kassidy walks into my office with a pinched smile on her beautiful face.

"What the hell happened with Dirk yesterday? Did you fuck him?" I ask her straight out.

Kassidy's brown cheeks don't hide the color that suddenly colors her brown skin. She nibbles her bottom lip and looks down at the floor wringing her hands together.

"Wha— What did Dirk tell you?" she asks finally finding my glare.

"I'm the one asking the damn questions Kassidy. Did you fuck Dirk before fucking me first?"

"Oh God! Let me explain—"

"How are you going to fucking explain you letting Dirk touch you before I had a chance to have you?"

Kassidy gasps and her eyes widen. "What do you mean? I don't know the rules. I'm sorry if I disappointed you. I'm just going to go. I knew this situation was a bad idea," she turns to walk away as tears build in her eyes.

"Wait!" I walk over and grasp her by the wrist. "Give me a chance to explain. I know you're not a slut. Far from it." I expel a long breath before continuing. I find you attractive, and I want to make love to you," I spit out. "Dirk and I both want you, but he wasn't supposed to have you until all of us got together to discuss an arrangement. He didn't play fair."

"I'm not a damn toy you know! You don't play fair either. We almost had sex—"

"We almost made love," I rectify.

I take in another deep breath to compose my words. What happens next is going to seal the deal between the three of us.

"What I feel for you is more than a flight of fancy." I drop my eyes to her soft, plump lips, and all I want to do is kiss her. "I want you, Kassidy. I can't sleep at night for thinking of all the ways I want to have you. Hell, I'm hard most of the time when I'm in your presence. Feel how much I need you," I take her hand and place it over my erection.

"Ahh," she says trying to pull her hand away, but I keep her hand in place and lean down to press my lips against hers.

Kassidy's mouth automatically opens, and I slide my tongue inside to parlay with hers.

"Can I have you? Can I take you the way I've been thinking about having you since the first day you walked into this office?" I reach around to give her plump ass a squeeze.

"Mm, how do you want me?" she moans.

"First answer my question."

"Yes," Kassidy whispers.

"Did Dirk or any other man ever fucked you back here?" I give her well-rounded ass another squeeze.

"Absolutely not!" she gasps in surprise. "I don't—"

"Allow me to be your first. I promise you; I'll make it good for you."

"Ahh, I'm not sure I'll like it."

"Trust me. You will."

"Let me make sure we aren't disturbed," I lock the office door and secure the room from prying eyes.

"You mean you want to do it here and now?"

"I want you totally naked and bent over my desk," I reply and walk over to open a desk drawer to remove a tube of lube.

"You keep lube in your desk drawer?"

"I've dreamed of this moment, so I came prepared."

A smile slipped on Kassidy's kissable lips. "I can't believe I'm doing this."

"I can. The chemistry between us is so thick, and I see the way you watch us when you think Dirk and I aren't looking. You want both of us. Admit it."

"I— I..."

"Don't lie Kass. There's nothing wrong with wanting us. Hell, we want you too. This is more than about sex. I want you to know that up front."

I sift through the drawer of my desk drawer. I place a dollop of gel in my hand and then I rub the gel over my shaft, making sure every inch of it is covered with the lubricant.

I direct Kassidy to bend over the desk and spread her legs, and I apply the cold gel between her ass cheeks. Then I massage her puckered hole by pushing my finger inside to spread the gel inside. I finger her ass for several seconds, helping her tight muscles to relax. When I feel she's ready, I place a hand at the small of Kassidy's back. She shivers, sucks in a sharp breath, and grabs the edge of the desk.

"Are you alright?" I ask quietly as I start to move one finger and then two in and out.

Kassidy pants and says, "Yes."

"I will go as slowly as you need me to go. I am going to be gentle with you, babe."

Kassidy glances back at me, I'm struck by her radiant beauty as I get ready to mount her.

I allow my cock to slide up and down Kassidy's crack a few times before I position myself to enter her. *Shit!* I can't fucking wait to get inside her virgin ass. I shove forward, slowing making my way past the tight muscles. Kassidy moans at the invasion of my cock.

"Do you need me to stop sweetheart?"

"Oh my! Don't stop," she says as I continue to push, slowly working my way in until I'm fully enveloped.

"Nikolai!" Kassidy cries out.

I place my hands on either side of Kassidy's waistline and set a rhythmic pace. I keep the pace slow, but I almost lose it when Kassidy grinds back against my crotch, meeting my thrusts and forcing me to go faster.

I grunt, bending down to place a kiss at her fragrant shoulder. "Damn you smell good. Fuck, you're gonna make me come before I want to," I growl.

"Mmm," she moans. I'm loving the way that Kassidy is responding to me.

I bend over again, wrapping one arm around her breast area and the other around her waist, and I bury my face in Kassidy's neckline to inhale. I bite back a guttural groan as my thrusts become more erratic and frantic.

Kassidy's breath catches when I begin pushing against her bottom. "You must relax and breathe, Kass."

Kassidy lets out a soft moan. "I've never done this before. I'm sorry if—"

"Sweetheart, you are giving me a gift, and I adore you for it. I promise I'll take it slow and make it good for you. Now push back on my cock and let me know at any point if you want me to stop."

Kassidy nods her head and pushes back against my massive head; I grit my teeth to keep from cumming. She's so damn tight and perfect. I allow my fingers to trail around her waistline down to her clit so I can stroke her slick nub as Kassidy rocks against my hard length. I groan, reveling in how slick she's becoming, and I feel an urgent need to push my erection in to the hilt.

Kassidy starts pressing her well-rounded ass back against me harder, and I push forward, feeling her muscles opening up to my invasion. "Fuck!" I grate out when my entire length slides in.

"Ooh!" she moans.

I pause to give her body time to process the fullness of my shaft embedded in her puckered hole. I murmur soothing words while caressing her back.

"How are you doing sweetheart?"

"Keep going— don't stop," Kassidy tells me looking over her shoulder. Her brown gaze attaches to mine; she gives me a seductive smile pressing back into my crotch at the same time.

"Shit. Woman, you're killing me here."

Kassidy wiggles her ass again as if to prove a point. I grip her waist and start rocking against her backside. She begins to roll in tempo with my plunges.

"Faster— harder," she whispers.

I pick up the tempo. Each of my thrusts drives me deeper inside her. Kassidy starts moaning. "Oh, Nikolai, that feels so good," she gasps taking even deeper into her hole.

A low guttural sound escapes me as my dick pushes entirely into her depths.

"Mine," I growl out repeatedly. "Tell me who do you belong to," I grit my teeth reveling in her tightness.

"I'm yours," she purrs.

"Fuck! You feel so tight, honey. I could stay inside you forever, so fucking good..." I lean over to cup the side of her face, urging her to turn. When her eyes meet mine once again, I plant my mouth against hers. Her mouth opens in a gasp, and I plunge my tongue within.

My cock keeps up a measured pace, pushing deeper inside her. Kassidy's juices flow more as I delve two fingers into her wet sex. I love the way her body responds to my touches. I'm totally taken by her passion. She's taken my heart and soul to places I've never wanted to go before. The feeling of Kassidy owning my heart makes my emotions soar like an eagle.

My plunges become longer with more urgency as her body grinds in unity with mine.

"Oh, Nikolai," she cries out, jerking her mouth from mine. "I'm yours," she moans.

I growl animalistically, "I belong to you and only you. I promise you are it for me." I reach between her thighs, playing with her clit again. Kassidy moans while tweaking her brown nipples.

"Cumming!" she gasps breathlessly.

Together, we ride out wave after wave of pleasure as the familiar heat began to build with fiery intensity between us.

My thrusts are fast and deep. My grunts and her moans become one melody. My shaft grows even larger just before I erupt inside her. Kassidy quivers and shudders beneath me. I hold her up by the waist least she collapses against the desk. "Fuck-- shit!" I grunt as I slam into Kassidy twice more before coming with a guttural groan through clenched teeth.

We slump onto the desk, spent, sweaty and panting.

I ease out of her once the orgasm subsides and turn

her in my arms. "I love you, Kassidy," I declare and plunge my eyes into hers.

Kassidy smiles and her brown eyes become glassy. "I love you, Nikolai," and before the words leave her lips, my mouth slams down on hers to seal our love for one another with a passionate kiss.

My mate is found at last!

CHAPTER EIGHTEEN

Nikolai

HAPPY BIRTHDAY KASSIDY

Club Summit was an upscale martini bar and lounge on MLK Street. Dirk and I had financed this club as well a few others around the city. I was glad that Kassidy's friend Anita had called the office and explained what she had planned for Kassidy. Dirk and I suggested using the Summit. Anita was glad to take us up on the offer of an upscale establishment such as this.

Dirk and I thought tonight was the perfect time to reveal our true nature to Kassidy as well.

In the past, this club had been our hunting ground, the place we searched for our mate, a place where we fed our hungers and lived out our wildest desires. Now, none of those things are necessary since Kassidy entered our lives and our true mate has been found.

Most of our pack hangs out at Summit on any given night. "Hey sweetheart, I want you to meet a few people. These people mean a lot to Dirk and me."

"Okay." Kassidy looks up at me and gives me a beautiful smile. Dirk steps on her other side. She turns her head and graces him with a smile.

"Nikolai, Dirk, it's great to see you," Alfred, a tall, well-built man from Kenya approached us. Alfred's eyes are as dark as midnight. He shakes my hand before doing the same to Dirk's. "Now tell me, is this the one?" Alfred asks with a charming smile as he takes in Kassidy between Dirk and I.

I notice a nervous look cloud Kassidy's eyes. I bend to brush the side of her neck with a soft kiss. A low growl leaves Dirk's throat, and he bends to brush a kiss against Kassidy's cheek.

"Alfred, I'd like you to meet Kassidy Davis, and yes, she belongs to us."

"I'm glad to meet you Miss Davis, especially on such a joyous occasion. Happy Birthday," Alfred extends his greeting by shaking her hand.

"Thank you Alfred, it's nice to meet you too," says Kassidy.

We made some more small talk before Dirk

motioned a group of women sitting at a table trying to get our attention.

"My friends are here," Kassidy's voice perks up as she notices her friends.

"Your friends are lively. I've made sure the bartender keeps the drinks flowing," Alfred says.

"Great," I reply, nodding at Alfred. Dirk and I lead Kassidy to the to the private area we had reserved for Kassidy's birthday celebration.

Happy birthday Kassidy!" Her friends jump up from the table hugging and extending her well wishes.

I can see a sheen of tears in Kassidy's eyes as she glances between her friends.

Once we are all settled, Kassidy makes quick introductions for Octavia and Leelayna. Dirk and I already knew Kassidy's friend Anita from a previous meeting.

"Kassidy you are glowing! I'm glad to see that you're so happy," Octavia says giving Dirk and I a curious glance as Kassidy sits between us.

Kassidy blushes when I take her hand in mine and bring it to my lips. Dirk takes Kassidy's other hand in his and does the same.

"Guys, please," Kassidy whispers.

Both Dirk and I chuckle. We look across the table at Octavia and Leelayna. Both of their mouths are agape in stunned surprise.

"Close your mouths my friends," Anita says with a

giggle. "Get used to Kassidy's boyfriends. This is the way she rolls now," Anita laughs, and give Dirk and I a wink.

"I hope that you two don't have a problem with that?" Dirk is the first one to reply.

"Hell no!" Octavia answers.

"If Kassidy has no problem, why should we?" Leelayna adds. She fans her face as if she became flustered.

"I'm so embarrassed," Kassidy whispers.

"You're so beautiful when you get all shy on us," Dirk says.

"She's more than beautiful," I agree. My cock hardens and stretches uncomfortably beneath my slacks.

Kassidy glances between the two of us and appreciation and happiness can be seen by the bright look in her eyes and the smile on her lips.

"This is too much but thank you guys for celebrating my birthday with me," Kassidy says softly.

"This idea belongs solely to Nikolai and Dirk," Anita admitted. "Anything I planned wouldn't be this expensive or fancy. Not on my budget."

"You two shouldn't have gone all out like this," Kassidy turns her glance to Dirk and me.

"Nothing is too much for you, sweetheart," I reply, and Dirk readily agrees.

Dinner was served. Dirk and I made sure to include all of Kassidy's favorites. Thanks to Anita who helped plan the menu.

After dinner more drinks are served.

Kassidy continues to laugh a lot with each Cosmopolitan she orders.

Kassidy's gaze continuously flits between Dirk and me.

"I hope you two don't mind if we steal your lady for a bit," Anita says, getting up from the table. Leelayna, and Octavia follow suit.

"Yeah! Let's dance," Octavia says.

"I...don't know," Kassidy stammers, I find her shyness adorable and just want to fuck her already.

"Don't be scared. It's your birthday," Anita says. "Let her up guys, you two will have her all to yourselves later," Anita wiggles her brows suggestively.

Kassidy giggles, as I scoot out of the way to let her up.

"Have fun. We will be watching," Dirk says as the women walk off toward the dance floor.

"Damn she's sexy as hell," I say watching Kassidy's ass jiggle as she walks away.

"Fuck yeah she is," Dirk concurs.

Our gazes follow Kassidy's every movement and delicious swirl of her wide hips. I have no doubt that Dirk is as entranced by her voluptuousness as I am. My eyes travel from the high heels on her feet and shift up her body to the carefree smile on her beautiful face. I move uncomfortably in my seat, wishing the movement will alleviate the pressure of my extending erection.

Fuck. The movement didn't help.

When one song ended, and another began Kassidy and her friends continued their dancing...

The wolf grumbles.

∾

Dirk

I observe Kassidy on the dance floor dancing and laughing with her friends. Nikolai watches too with a beer in his hand.

"She's so beautiful isn't she?" Nikolai asks.

"Yes, she's more beautiful than any woman I know. Both inside and out." I pick up my beer and take a healthy swig without taking my eyes from Kassidy.

"How do you think she will handle what we tell her tonight?" I ask Nikolai.

"I think Kassidy is a smart, mature, and open minded woman. I want to believe that she's able to accept and be part of our Alpha triad."

I agree. Kassidy is the ideal mate for us. I didn't

want to admit it, but I knew it from when she walked into my office.

"Yeah," Nikolai chuckles. "I'm glad you finally came to your senses and accepted what I knew all along."

We knew choosing a human mate may cause us some challenges but Nikolai and I are up for the task.

"Have you thought about how her body will react after we mark her? I have, and I don't—"

"There is always the question of what if Kassidy's body is strong enough to make it through the change. We must remain positive that she is. I don't think we would have been drawn to her otherwise," Nikolai cut me off.

"The pack will stand behind us, and have already given us their blessing," Nikolai adds. I nod as I glance at Nikolai reaffirming that we made the right decision before turning my glance back to Kassidy.

She looks so happy and that makes me happy. She's still dancing and laughing with her friends. My cock hardens with thoughts of what the night will bring once we get her alone.

Nikolai raise his hand to a passing waitress and grabs us two more beers. The night passes but my friend and I grow more inpatient...

After a while, I had enough.

175

"Are you thinking what I'm thinking?" Dirk asks before I speak.

"Let's go claim our woman," I reply and we stand and head towards the dance floor.

"Yikes!" Kassidy yells in surprise, I grab her around the waist and pull her to me. Dirk gets behind her and we make a delicious sandwich out of her.

"I need to taste you." I bend bringing my lips close to her ear so she could hear me over the music.

"Not here," Kassidy softly says, glancing up at me.

"I insist." My voice grow more powerful, "But you're right. I will taste all of you later and that's a promise."

Kassidy sighs and for the rest of the night I restrain from taking her right there on the dance floor for the entire crowd to see.

After a couple hours of celebrating, Dirk's inner wolf growls. "I've had enough. It's time to claim our mate."

"I agree." I hurry Kassidy to make her goodbyes. She's looking perplexed and flushed by the time we lead her out of there.

Groaning low, we all get into the back seat of the limo Dirk and I hired. The driver already knows the deal. We would be going to my home. To my bedroom. With the humongous bed, more than big enough for the three of us.

"Tonight you become ours, Kassidy. Are you ready?" I ask.

"Ahh-- yes," she nods... although slowly.

~

Nikolai

LATER THAT NIGHT

Once inside, my tongue intertwines with Kassidy's. Dirk supports Kassidy's back, but I find comfort in her soft curvaceous body as she leans towards me. Our tongues swirl and tangle. Her aroma cloaks me, causing my wolf to claw the way through to the surface. I revel in the differences between our bodies. I'm rock-solid, and her softness continues to draw me in.

"Do you want us Kassidy?" I mutter.

"I want you both-- I need you both. So much," she moans into my mouth.

A twin low growl emerges from my throat and Dirk's.

"Bed, now," Dirks says with a gruff tone.

"Fuck yeah," my tone is equally desire filled and growly.

Slowly, we strip Kassidy of her clothes before tearing off our own.

Moaning, Kassidy sifts her fingers through my hair and gives it a hard tug. "Oh my God, Dirk, I need you inside me now."

I kiss my way back up her curvy body, dipping my tongue inside her deep navel to give it a swirl before sliding back up to mesh my lips with hers. I growl ferally. Kassidy jumps back. I don't hide the fine hair growing on my flesh. My eyes are now the wolf's.

"Wha.. What?"

"Don't be afraid Kassidy," Dirk comes around to face her. Do you trust us?"

"Just know we will never hurt you. That's a promise," I say.

Kassidy gulps but nods.

"Alright. But don't run sweetheart. What you are about to see may be unsettling, but this is our true nature. And above all, remember that you are our mate. This is our destiny."

Dirk and I change our appearance to our wolf forms, but not completely. That will come in time. We remain upright, our eyes glow golden, light colored hair dusks my skin, while dark hair coats Dirk's.

"Oh my fucking—" Kassidy's eyes bulge, and her mouth gapes open. "I knew you two were different. I had no idea this was it, but I knew!"

"Are you afraid?" Dirk asks.

"I'm more in shock, but for some reason, I'm not

afraid of you. Somehow I feel more drawn to you. I don't know what it is," she ends by saying.

"You are meant for us. Now the question is, do you want to be ours until the end of time?" Dirk asks.

"Yes," Kassidy didn't hesitate. I knew she was brave. I knew she was strong enough to accept us for who and what we really are.

"You are so damn hot sweetheart. I can't wait to get my cock inside you," I reply, feeling an inkling of pride and ownership settling deep within my soul.

"Yes. Ours!" Dirk's voice roars.

~

Dirk

I bend and lick the side of Kassidy's neck. The smell of her has me wanting to crawl inside of her. I crave every part of this woman like I need air to breathe. My heart thunders against my chest with each caress of my lips.

"Mm," Kassidy moans just before Nikolai cups her face in his hands and slams his mouth against his.

"Shit," I growl. I need to be inside Kassidy's sweet pussy. *Now*. I need to take possession of her heart, mind, and soul.

I position myself behind her and trail my hands

down her soft belly. My cock pries itself between the plush cheeks of her ass.

"Bed!" Kassidy cries out, and my wolf answers. Scooping her up in my arms, I place her in the middle of the bed. Nikolai and I position ourselves on each side of our beautiful mate.

"I told you I would taste you," Nikolai says, getting to his knees. He maneuvers himself into position, prodding her thick succulent thighs apart as he closes the gap between them. "Your pussy smells so good," Nikolai bends and gives it a whiff.

I grow harder looking at the glistening pinkness of Kassidy's wetness. It contrasts against her dark brown skin.

"Oh my! I want—" Kassidy trails off.

"Oh, bay, Dirk and I are going to take care of you." My hands stroke her breasts and give her brown nipples a pinch. My palms continue their excursion, down to her belly. I imagine Kassidy carrying our pups one day soon.

"I can smell your desire." Kassidy whines at my words. "Your sweet pussy and ass is begging for your mates."

Nikolai growls as his tongue dips between Kassidy sweet folds. My turn will come to taste her delicacy soon.

In the meantime, I bend to take a budded nipple

into my mouth. My tongue swirls and tantalizes the hardened bud.

Each swipe of my tongue against her nipple brings a moan from Kassidy's plump, kissable mouth. Each swipe against her clit by Nikolai's tongue does the same.

Kassidy whimpers and angles her hips, begging for more.

My cock lengthens further, and my wolf growls demanding me to take her.

Soon—soon she would be mine. No, Kassidy would be ours. Completely.

Kassidy

My pussy clenches, tightening with each swipe of Nikolai's tongue.

My thoughts are filled with inconceivable desire. My mind is in shock. I never knew wolves existed. I've watched Teen Wolf, and other television shows on the subject, but I never would have suspected that they really existed; until now. That makes me wonder, do other things exist—like vampires. *Oh my God!*

My mind turns from my thoughts when Nikolai's fingers join his talented tongue. His fingers plunge as his tongue swipes up and down my wet slit. My pleasure doubles as Dirk caresses my body and sucks on my nipples.

I whine and grind against Nikolai's mouth.

"More," I cry, tightening my hand in his hair.

Nikolai chuckles. "You want more? Do you want me in your sweet pussy and Dirk in that delectable ass of yours? Hmm?"

I whimper. "Yes. I need you both inside me."

"I'm going to taste that sweet pussy first," Dirk grumbles. He gets up, nudging Nikolai out the way. Dirk settles between my thighs.

I can feel his hot breath brush against my inner thigh. Dirk wastes no time lapping at my wet heat. He softly kisses to my wetness. "You do taste sweet," Dirk growls and sucks my nub between his lips. I cry out as pleasure ricochets through my entire being.

I feel a bite at my nipple and almost jump from the bed. Nikolai chuckles and swipes his tongue across my nipple to soothe the sting.

"Do you like Dirk eating your pussy?" Nikolai asks.

I whimper but nod my head yes.

"So beautiful," Dirk mutters against my mound.

"Stunning," Nikolai agrees.

"Mine," Dirk growls.

"Ours," comes Nikolai's answering growl.

With their words, I cum like never before. Heat waves of pleasure wash over me from head to toe.

"Y-Yes!" I cry out as the orgasm vibrates and settles down to a slow thump.

"Sweet." Dirk rises and settles against my back as he and Nikolai change sides. Now, Nikolai's back is at my front.

"Are you ready for us sweetheart?" Nikolai asks.

"Yes," I moan.

I turn and see Dirk reach over to a nearby table for a bottle of lubricant. He squirts a generous amount and lathers it over his massive erection. Nikolai lies flat on his back and directs me to straddle him. I then feel Dirk at my forbidden hole squirting me with lubricant.

Dirk's finger dips in stretching me. I moan, and a few seconds later, I grit my teeth as Dirk places more fingers inside my anus, stretching me even more.

"Look at me sweetheart," Nikolai urges me just as his hard length taps at my slick entrance.

"Put me inside you. Now," he orders.

"Ahh, yes!" I cry out when Nikolai thrusts deep inside my wet core to the hilt. I can feel the inside of my inner core stretching to accommodate Nikolai's thickness and length.

"Fuck," Nikolai grumbles. Nikolai pushes into me, setting a rhythm.

"That feels so good. Oh, yes," I whine.

"Your pussy is so fucking good sweetheart. Dirk get in her ass," Nikolai adds.

My body trembles when I feel Dirk's impressive length at my back. He pushes in bit by bit, stretching me to accommodate him. The sting is unbelievable but so is the pleasure. My desire burns hotter the more my lovers feed me their cocks.

Dirk whispers sweet words and nibbles on my neck, trying to soothe his entrance. Nikolai's thrusts are sweet torture. My pussy throbs with pleasure. I tremble, once Dirk is inside my ass to the hilt. My lovers set a rhythm. When Nikolai pushes back, Dirk thrusts forward. Pain and pleasure collide.

My pleasure is soon outweighing the pain, and my desire is growing with another glorious orgasm.

"Mm," I moan. "Feels so good. Harder."

My guys don't make me wait. They fuck me hard.

Dirk's hand slips between Nikolai's and my joined body, and his fingers flick against my swollen nub.

"Cum for us," Nikolai grits out between clenched teeth.

My back arches, my head slumps forward-- then I explode. My heart thumps erratically against my chest.

The fiery heat of bliss washes over every nerve of my body from my explosive release. My entire body trembles, my walls are still clenching.

Nikolai raises his head, and his mouth captures my nipple; more bliss is my reward.

Eyes locked on me, Nikolai asks, "Are you ready to become ours completely, Kassidy?"

"Yes," I reply.

Dirk growls in pleasure. "I'm ready to cum," he admits as his shaft throbs in my ass.

Yes! My heart rejoices. I want to feel both of my lovers' essence deep inside me.

Soon, both Nikolai and Dirk howl out in blissful pleasure as their dicks jerk and spasm inside of me. Their hot seed embeds deep, and I feel myself cumming again and again.

The sounds of our sweaty, slapping bodies fill the room; their growly snarls mix with my whines of explicit joy as their cocks slide against one another, the thin tissues of my pussy were the only thing to separate them.

"Now, Dirk," Nikolai growls.

I felt both their wolves' canines sink into each of my shoulders. The piercing pain slices my skin. I even smell the coppery smell of my blood float around the room.

A swell of blinding pleasure consumes me. Our intertwined bodies are as one, and I could feel my bond grow with them by monstrous proportions.

Now, I am soulfully tied to my two sexy alpha

wolves forever. My vision clouds and I whine as their fangs recede. They lap the remaining blood from my shoulders. I slump forward, and Nikolai cradles me to his hard muscular chest.

I take in a deep breath. The room is filled with the smell of sex and the remnants of the coppery smell of blood.

"Now you are ours," Dirk says, pulling out of me with a wet plop.

"Yours," I agreed as my men rolled over to place me solidly between them.

"Delightfully ours from this time forward," Nikolai agrees.

My strong Alpha mates. I am theirs, and they are mine. I would have it no other way.

EPILOGUE

Kassidy

y two bosses and I are still together, but they are no longer my bosses. They are my life-long mates. Dirk and Nikolai offered me an arrangement. They both gave me a proposition to move in with them. Dirk and Nikolai agreed to build a home for me that the three of us will soon share. Until then, I will live a week with Nikolai and then trade off to Dirk. They both declare their love and loyalty to only me. The arrangement gives me the love, and romantic interaction I crave while still feeding into the other aspects of our relationship. I agree, under the condition that they still share me often because I adore them both. There was a time when there was only me. Now it's the three of us, and I feel more complete than I ever have before. I feel worshipped being loved and cherished by the two men who have proven to me repeatedly how much I am valued.

It's been a couple of weeks since Nikolai and Dirk bit me and asked me to live with them, and it has been two of the best weeks of my life. Each day with my lovers is spent loving and feeling more cherished than the last. I didn't have to lift a finger with the move. Both of my take charge men took care of everything. They even hired a packing company to take care of my things in my apartment. Thank heavens my lease is going to be up in a month, but of course, they took care of that too.

We almost came into a disagreement when they wanted me to give up my job. I am independent and don't want to be treated like a kept woman, and I made that very clear. When I threatened to work somewhere else, Nikolai and Dirk both agreed they wanted to keep me on my present job.

Don't get me wrong, I realize we will have our arguments and ups and downs. I won't win every case every time, but that's okay. I love making up with my two alphas.

Now, as I lie with the two loves of my life, I know that I no longer just have them in my dreams— because it doesn't get any realer than this.

"Damn it, Kassidy, you make me crazy," Dirk's

voice grumbles. My eyes switch from Nikolai to Dirk, and I plunge my brown gaze into his blue depths. I let out a moan thinking about two magnificent cocks hard and ready for my mouth.

I'm incredibly nervous, but also very turned on by the feelings rushing through me. The demanding sounds of both Nikolai's and Dirk's voices send electrical shocks straight to my core.

"Raise your ass a little bit more," Dirk growls.

Nikolai places a pillow underneath my hips to assist me with the position.

I can't believe how lucky I got to be in a loving relationship with my two alphas. I'm ass up and face down readying myself to be ravished by not one, but two of the sexiest men I've ever met. If I'm dreaming, I never want to wake up.

I widen my thighs and lean further over the pillows; I place my arms on the bed and lie my head against them. I wonder what they have planned for me. I wonder if I will actually be able to take on two of them together or one at a time... My body is trembling with desire.

My skin tingles at the thought of the two men that I love doing delicious things to my body. I desire to please them as well. All these thoughts are running rapidly through my head, causing a nervous feeling to rush through my system.

"We got you, sweetheart," Nikolai's deep sexy voice penetrates my thoughts. It's as if he read my inner thoughts. He traces a hand up and down my inner thigh. I can hear the sound of a zipper sliding down. Peering over my shoulder, I can see a shirtless Dirk is now divesting himself of his slacks and underwear.

I gulp, staring at the vast expanse of his chest. Dirk's rippling abs and the deep lust that's radiating from his eyes causes my legs to quiver. More wet heat blooms deep in my core from his blatant perusal. Their eyes on me makes me wetter and hotter. All this, and I haven't yet been penetrated.

Suddenly, Nikolai stops touching me, and I hear the scrape of another zipper as he takes a step back. I crane my neck to see Nikolai getting out of his clothes. My breathing is rapid as is my heartbeat. The bass like sound of my erratically beating heart, sounds like a drum beat in rhythmic succession with my heart.

Another shiver passes through me as both men approach. I take in a fortifying breath then exhale, waiting, and wondering what will happen next. Tiny bumps from my shivering break out over my brown skin.

My clit throbs and my dusty brown nipples harden. They pulse in rhythm with my slick core.

Everything seems to happen at once. Dirk slides

beneath my body. His face is in direct alignment with my mound. Nikolai positions himself behind me, settling his strong hands at my waist.

"Oh my God!" I cry out when Nikolai bends and places a kiss directly on my rounded ass cheek. "Mmm," I moan when Dirk's hand settles on my upper thigh.

"I want to taste your sweetness," he growls out in a gruff voice.

"Yes!" I scream as his tongue swipes against my wet sex.

My breath becomes lodged in my chest as all these feelings inhabit my body at once. I can feel Nikolai's hot, wet tongue tracing patterns all over my ass.

Nikolai's hands and mouth are all over my ass cheeks. I scream with pleasure when he spreads my cheeks and delves his tongue into a forbidden spot that's never been touched or tantalized in that way. Nikolai's tongue wiggles into my tight hole, and he begins to lick. I don't believe he is really licking me there, and I can't believe that I'm enjoying it.

Dirk's tongue is beginning to swirl and plunge inside my slick heat. My entire body is shaking from pure hot pleasure. The feelings coursing through me become too much, then not enough. Nikolai kisses his way up my spine. His hands reach around me, grasps my bountiful breasts, squeezing and plucking at my pointy nipples.

"Ooh," I croon, the manipulation of my breasts combine with the erotic shocks zigzagging through my pussy as Dirk devours me below.

Nikolai pulls away, and I become unsettled; but not for long as Dirk's plunging his tongue into my heated core intensifies, the clicking noise of a cap opening penetrates my foggy brain. I jump when I feel something cold and wet on the back entrance of my ass. I'm guessing it's lube.

Suddenly, Nikolai's finger is pressed firmly against my back entrance, to plunge deep. I shudder from the fullness, and my muscles automatically tighten, trying to dislodge his questing fingers.

"Relax, sweetheart," Nikolai's says. "I promise you will enjoy it. Open for me. Let me in. I'm preparing you for my cock."

"Yes!" my inner goddess growls.

Dirk takes that moment to clamp down on my clit, my back entrance muscles, and Nikolai's fingers slide home. A delicious, forbidden thrill settles over me. My hips begin moving on their own accord, seeking out a release that is attempting to overtake me. Before tonight, I never would have thought this possible. Nikolai, Dirk, and I; us as a whole becoming one big ball of sexual energy.

I want more. I want all that these handsome men have to give me. Dirk bites down on my clit again. The bite of pain makes my clit pulse. I begin to buck wildly, and erratically. Nikolai's fingers plunge deep into me.

"Cum for us," he demands against my ear.

Pressure begins radiating deep inside my core. My ass is tight around Nikolai's fingers, my pussy is filled with Dirk's plunging, swirling tongue. The pleasure coursing through my entire body is sensually intense. Nature takes its course, and I explode.

Dirk withdraws his fingers slowly from me, and I want to fill the loss instantly. Dirk eases out from beneath me and changes position. My eyes latch on to the impressive length and girth of his shaft. He reaches for the pillow beneath me and eases beneath my body, this time his erection is aligned with my mound.

"We are going to make love to you. We want to show you how good it can be between the two of us." Dirk gazes up into my eyes. "Do you trust me baby— do you trust us?"

I nod my head in an up and down motion.

"We need to hear the words darling," Nikolai comes back again, this time with placing his long, smooth, stiff erection at my forbidden entrance. He pushes in slowly, never rushing the process. Once inside, Nikolai begins to stroke in and out-out and in.

My legs widen when Dirk plunges inside my core.

I'm stuffed tight from both ends. We soon developed a rhythm that puts us in sync. I can feel my desire building. These two glorious men, both inside me, claiming me, making me theirs, fills me with so much love.

Each man is giving me themselves slowly, stretching me beyond the point of sweet pain and intense pleasure. Between these two, I'm unraveling and come into a realm I never knew existed until now.

Nikolai and Dirk are right there with me, thrusting into me fast and hard. I freely and willingly give myself to them both. It's the most sensual thing I've ever experienced. I'm theirs in every conceivable way possible, to do with as they want to. I know that whatever pleasures them will undoubtedly make me happy too. I love and trust them both. Deeply—now and forever.

THE END

ACKNOWLEDGMENTS

First, thank you God for everything.

Thank you to my family who put up with my writing habits at odd hours of the night and mornings.

A special acknowledgment to Carmi, a loyal reader who pushes me in my writing. Thanks to my book cover designer, Bryant Sparks for the great cover, my editor, Joseph Editorial Services, and my book formatter, Tammy Clarke.

Thanks to everyone who has helped my rough draft of a story shine better than it did before.

ABOUT THE AUTHOR

Theresa Hodge is an Alabama native - loving mother, wife, sister, aunt and friend. She is at her best when she is able to bring happiness to others. This author loves to read almost as much as she loves to write fictional stories. She finds writing therapeutic at times, especially during the loss of her oldest sister from breast cancer, which birthed her "Ask Me Again" Series. This was her first but this compilation led to her writing several other books. These book's includes her best-selling Noelle's Rock series among many others.

Additionally, Theresa has a love affair with poetry. She began writing poetry at an early age and it served as a catalyst for her growth as a writer.

If Theresa can bring a smile to your face and encourage someone else along her journey, she considers it a blessing beyond measure.

KEEP IN TOUCH

twitter.com/Poetic__Life?s=o9
Like Page:

www.facebook.com/askmeagainromanceseries

Instagram
Instagram.com/gemini2goddess

Goodreads:
www.goodreads.com/author/show/
6927856.Theresa_Hodge

BookBub:
www.bookbub.com/profile/theresa-hodge

Pinterest:
www.pinterest.com/terehod

Newsletter Sign-up:
amazon.us9.list-manage.com/subscribe?u=
ffde15be91b185d57d934a65c&id=1f6b614090

Website:
www.amazon.com/Theresa-Hodge/e/B00J53PB3E

terehod.wixsite.com/mysite-1

Made in the USA
Monee, IL
28 February 2020